Mail Order GROOM

DANA WAYNE

A Division of Y&R Enterprises, LLC
PO Box 2283
Lindale, TX 75771

Interior Book design by Champagne Formats
Cover design by Just Write.Creations

Library of Congress Control Number Data
Wayne, Dana
Mail Order Groom / Wayne, Dana.
Historical—Romance—Fiction.2. Western—Romance—Fiction.
Fiction. | BISAC: FICTION / Romance / Historical. | Fiction / Romance / Western.
Library of Congress Control Number: 2017936610

ISBN 978-1-940460-871

www.danawayne.com
www.yandrpublishing.com

PRAISE FOR MAIL ORDER GROOM

"Stories in the Old West are legion about mail order brides, brought to a vast, empty landscape to bring a sense of order and comfort, perhaps even love, to lonely men fighting for survival in a country that refuses to be tamed or civilized. But what happens when a beautiful and desperate woman learns she must find a husband or lose her ranch? Only Dana Wayne knows, and, just like her defiant heroine in Mail Order Groom, she has the heart, the spirit, the courage to weave a story not quite like anything you have ever read before. Dana Wayne's characters don't live on a printed page. They live in your heart for a long time."

Caleb Pirtle, Author
Ambrose Lincoln Series

"Meet ranchers' daughter, Emma Marshall. She's tough, capable, and about to have her world turned upside-down. Through the story-telling mastery of award winning author Dana Wayne, we find Emma head to head with her dying father. He wants her married. She wants no part of it. A jean-wearing, cattle-herding, headstrong woman, she fights for her independence. Tyler Roundtree is about to change her mind. A spark ignites when the new foreman arrives, but will that fire blaze or does the black-hearted town lawyer have a different outcome in mind? This novel takes us back to the days when a woman's place wasn't out branding cattle or building fences; but, Emma is no ordinary woman. Take a ride with Dana Wayne as she tells a tale of love and deceit in the wild-west."

Patty Wiseman, Author
The Velvet Shoe Series

PRAISE FOR SECRETS OF THE HEART

"Walk down the path with Dana Wayne as she blends heartbreak and despair with hope and love."

Patty Wiseman, Author

"One of the most endearing books I have read, one to re-read over and over again."

Marichus Real, Story Cartel

"Dana Wayne has written a romantic winner that touches all of the emotions and touches them with love and compassion."

Book Editor

"…a finely plotted and beautifully written novel about true love and second chances."

Jack Mangus, Readers Favorite Reviewer

CHAPTER
One

East Texas, Spring, 1878

Y OU'VE GOT THIRTY DAYS TO FIND A HUSBAND OR I'LL FIND *one for you.*

Her father's recent ultimatum bounced around Emma's head like a hail stone, causing her concentration to falter.

"Miss Marshall? Are you all right?"

John Ralston, the cattleman she came to Ft. Worth to see, watched with anxious eyes.

"My apologies, Mr. Ralston. I guess I am still tired from the trip."

He nodded. "I understand. It's a long trip from Bakersville." He motioned for the waitress to refill their coffee. "I wasn't aware of your father's illness until I received your telegram. I have to say, finding a woman such as yourself interested in my Herefords is unusual."

"My father told me about them after your meeting last year. I can't wait to see how they fare. How long has your herd been here? Has our finicky weather had any adverse effects on them?"

The next hour flew by, and when it ended, Emma was the proud owner of a Hereford bull and two heifers.

After Ralston left, she lingered over her coffee and savored the success of having completed not only the purchase of new breeding stock, but negotiating the sale of the herd they would bring in next month. The new purchase would be picked up then and driven back to the ranch.

He trusts me to negotiate the sale of our cattle but not to run the ranch. The smile of accomplishment faded. No matter how hard she tried, Rafe Marshall believed only a man could run Twin Oaks Ranch.

Their last conversation, still a vivid memory, played out in her mind.

"I'm dyin', girl. Doc sez I ain't got much longer. I gotta know Twin Oaks will be in good hands."

"By *good*, you mean *male*." It took tremendous effort to keep the hurt gnawing her insides from showing in her voice. "*That's* what you really mean."

He sighed and squinted. "We been over this time and again. Ranchin' ain't woman's work. You're almost twenty-six. You should've been married years ago with a passel o' young'uns for me to spoil, not runnin' round in britches and boots tryin' to do a man's job."

"I've no wish to get married, Papa, I've told you so repeatedly." *Because being married is like being property. No voice, no face, no freedom.*

He ignored her comment. "Tom Blakely over to the Lazy

B would be good."

She stared in disbelief. "You can't be serious. He's ancient. At least forty!"

"Or maybe Hank Walker."

His mention of the local attorney made her skin crawl. Hank made no secret of his interest and was prone to show up unannounced requesting she accompany him for a ride or the occasional dance.

She never accepted. He never gave up.

"I wouldn't marry Hank Walker if he were the last man on earth."

Rafe blew out a noisy breath. "I mean what I say." Pale blue eyes bored into hers. "Find a husband in thirty days or I'll find one for you."

"And if I don't?"

He paused. "Then Twin Oaks goes to my brother in Ft. Worth when I die."

That thought brought her back to the present with a jolt. Would he really give away her home, force her marry someone she didn't love? How could a father do something like this do his only child?

The coffee she enjoyed a moment ago turned sour in her stomach. Heart filled with despair, she adjusted the bow on her bonnet, and rose from the table. The desk clerk here at The El Paso Hotel mentioned earlier a new mercantile recently opened down the block. She decided it would be a great place to find gifts for her two best friends, Sarah and Mable.

Preoccupied with her father's dictate, she collided with a cowboy walking by as she exited the hotel.

Without conscious thought, she grabbed for his arms to keep from tumbling down the steps to the muddy street below. Her fingers clutched strong muscles that tightened beneath them, sending unexpected tingles up her arms.

Large hands grabbed her waist, their warmth adding to the unfamiliar sensations coursing through her.

"Whoa, there, ma'am."

His soft drawl caused gooseflesh on her arms and her gaze jerked up to his face. Eyes, grey as a storm cloud, caused her breath to hitch.

He hesitated, then set her away from him and tipped his hat. "Excuse me, ma'am. I wasn't watching where I was going." With a quick nod, he walked away.

She stood immobile for several heartbeats, then looked down at her gloved hands, surprised at the warm tingles lingering there.

The memory of those hypnotic eyes followed her the rest of the day and into the night, disrupting her sleep and making her irritable for the long journey home.

By the time she arrived two days later, she was accustomed to their frequent invasion of her thoughts.

Since her father expected an immediate report, she didn't bother to freshen up before entering his room. She removed her bonnet and gloves as she took her usual chair beside his bed. "How are you feeling today?"

"How did it go? Any problems?"

She took a breath before replying. "No, there were no problems. Mr. Ralston agreed to the terms we discussed before I left."

"I expect so since I had Leo telegraph ahead."

Her heart sank. "I should have known. I'm a woman and therefore can't do anything without a man to help me."

He clamped his jaw and remained silent.

She stood and paced around the room. "I can do anything any man on this ranch can do, even better than some, and I've handled everything just fine these last few months you've been sick."

"The only reason the men do what you tell them is because I'm still here." He struggled to sit up, then sank back on the pillows when his strength faded. "They won't listen to you when I'm dead, and everything I spent my life building will be gone."

She turned and faced him, emerald eyes stinging with unshed tears. "I don't understand how you can think so little of me."

"Don't start that nonsense again, girl, I – "

"My name is Emma Rose. Not Girl!" She hated it when he referred to her as *girl* as though she didn't even rate being called by her name. She lowered her voice. "I'm sorry your son died with my mother. I'm sorry I'm not a man." She paused a moment to gather her composure. "I finally realize no matter what I do, it will never be enough. You want me to find a husband…fine…I'll find a husband."

She stormed out of his room, slamming the door shut behind her, ignoring his demand they discuss the new foreman due to arrive soon.

Rafe glowered at the closed door, annoyed with himself for once again making a mess of things, but he lacked the time for tact and diplomacy.

He was dying.

He accepted that. What distressed him more than

the disease eating away his body one bite at a time was the thought of his only child being left alone when he died. His beautiful, smart, and head-strong Emma Rose who had the misfortune to inherit the predominant traits of both her parents. Tall and beautiful like her mother, with tobacco colored hair and emerald eyes that flashed with life or cut you to the bone, and headstrong and independent like her father.

I should've done a better job with her, made sure she knew how to be a woman. Now, it's too late.

Devastated by the death of his wife when Emma was ten, he'd closed himself off for years. By the time he realized his mistake, the void between them appeared insurmountable.

When was the last time I told her I loved her? How proud I am of her? I just want her to be happy. His brow furrowed as he tried to remember the last time he saw her smile. It shamed him to admit he couldn't.

She loved the ranch and it belonged to her. He had no intention of leaving it to his worthless brother; he merely used the threat as incentive to get her to at least look for a husband.

He wanted her to take his concerns seriously. Despite what she thought, he suffered no reservations about her ability to run the place. The men respected her and she worked hard to earn and keep their respect.

What killed his soul was the thought she would grow old alone.

Like him.

He blew out a breath and drummed his fingers on his chest. *I should've told her about the posters and the ad in the Ft. Worth paper.*

CHAPTER
Two

Tyler Roundtree entered the Broken Spur Saloon and paused. Hooded gray eyes scanned the room, marked the position of each customer as well as doors and windows before he sauntered toward the worn oak bar. He angled to the right, his back to the wall, where the door and room remained visible.

The bartender, a huge barrel of a man, his face a mass of wrinkles, gaze heavy lidded and bored, wiped the counter as he approached. "What'll it be, mister?"

"Whiskey. The good stuff. Leave the bottle."

Ty grabbed the items, dropped coins on the bar, and moved to a table in the corner. He sipped the potent drink, enjoying the pungent bite as it slid down his throat to warm his near empty belly. Brim of his worn Stetson pulled low, he missed nothing around him.

Not for the first time, he asked himself why he had

accepted the job at Twin Oaks two weeks ago. The fact that Henry Owens talked him into it spoke volumes for their friendship. They served together in the war and Henry returned home and married Sarah five years ago.

Ty still searched for a home to return to.

On Ty's last visit to the Owens ranch, Henry advised him the Marshall's foreman died after being thrown from a wild mustang. With Henry's recommendation and encouragement, Ty applied for the job and here he sat, putting off the moment he would meet his new employer with a mixture of dread and anticipation.

Laughter from a nearby table drew his gaze toward it.

"What on earth made you think you had a chance with her, Lucky?" The question came from a young cowboy, slender as a reed, hair the color of iron ore rocks, whose prominent Adams apple bobbed wildly when he spoke. "Hell, she'd eat you alive and spit out your bones!"

The one referred to as Lucky ducked his head and grunted. "Yeah, well, at least she didn't kick my ass like she did the feller from the Bentley place."

His comment brought another round of laughter from the group.

Lucky snorted. "He should 'a known better than to try and kiss her. She's prickly as a cactus."

His cohorts bobbed their heads in silent agreement.

"You gonna give it a try, Slim?"

The red-headed cowboy spoke up. "Hell no. I mean, she's purty as a speckled pup when she fixes up, but I got no desire to bed a woman who is tall as me, can probably out shoot, out cuss, *and* out ride me."

More nods from the table.

"I mean, who wouldn't want Twin Oaks? Three thousand acres of the best water and grazing around. Old man Marshall done a fine job with it. Too bad he raised her to be a boy 'stead of a girl."

"Sure is a shame," said Lucky, "it is for a fact."

Slim glanced at Ty. "Say, mister, you here to try your luck?"

Ty looked up but didn't reply.

"You here cause of them posters?" Slim shook his head. "I can't believe Old Man Marshall had notices stuck up all over the place looking for her a husband."

Ty's curiosity overrode his natural aloofness. "She that bad?"

A chorus of "Hell no's" greeted his question.

"She can be right pretty," offered one cowboy, "slim, kinda tall, though, brownish hair and crazy green eyes."

"Yeah," said Lucky, "it's like they can see right through a man."

"Got a smart mouth, though," declared another from group. "Don't know a woman's place."

"Yeah," said Lucky, "she runs Twin Oaks like a man. Even wears britches!"

"And that's bad?" Ty's question held a note of sarcasm the group didn't appear to notice.

"Well, yeah," said the leader of the group, "a woman should be doing woman stuff like cookin' and havin' babies, not brandin' cattle."

"I help out from time to time," offered the man nearest Slim. "Last year I seen her wrestle this bull calf to the ground and castrate him right then and there."

Lucky actually shuddered. "A woman ought not do that."

Ty's attention swung to the front door where the squeak of rusty hinges announced another arrival.

A man entered and stopped, surveying the room with a commanding air of self-confidence. He wore a black derby hat cocked over one heavy brow and an unlit cigar protruded from the corner of thin lips. He wore a dark suit and tie even though the Texas heat steadily climbed. He stood about six feet-tall, with broad shoulders and an arrogant swagger. He strode toward the cowboys' table and stopped. He removed the cigar from his mouth and sniffed it, disdainful smile aimed at Lucky. "I hear things didn't go well today."

Lucky avoided looking at the man, a bright flush on his cheeks. "So what?"

The man patted him on the shoulder, gaze shifting to Ty as he spoke. "Told you it was a waste of time. Emma's mine. You all best remember that."

The hair on the back of Ty's neck tingled like it did the time he walked up on a rattlesnake ready to strike.

The man eyed him a moment, then stepped forward. "Haven't seen you around here before."

"Haven't been here before."

"Name's Hank Walker." He held out his hand.

Ty eyed the hand but made no move to shake. "Tyler Roundtree."

"Well, Mr. Roundtree I –"

"No mister, just Tyler."

"I see. Well, Tyler, what's your business here in Bakersville?"

Ty sipped his whiskey, right hand dropping to grip the handle of the Colt strapped to his leg. "Don't see as how my business is any of yours."

Walker's smile never reached his eyes. "If you're here about Emma Marshall, you can leave now."

The last thing he needed or wanted was to get in the middle of someone else's problem. Already, this job had earmarks of trouble in spades. He had no doubt he'd just met an adversary…one with his eye on Emma Marshall, who he assumed to be his new employer's daughter. But, he promised Henry he would take this job until they found someone else, and he would not break his word. Plus, he didn't like Walker on sight and had no qualms about provoking him.

"What if I am?"

"As I said, you can leave now."

"And if I don't care to?"

Chair legs scrapped against the rough wood floor as Slim and his companions moved toward the door.

"I'm the Marshalls' attorney." Walker pulled his coat open to show he carried no gun. "I have their best interest in mind."

Ty studied the man intently. *Evil eyes.* "That include Miss Marshall? You looking out for her best interest, too?"

Walker's nostrils flared and his jaw tightened. When he spoke, his voice was cold and flat. "She's none of your concern."

He sipped his whiskey. "Well, since I'm the new foreman, and she's the boss's daughter, I reckon she *is* my concern."

Walker flinched, gaze darting around to see who might have heard him. "Since when?"

"Since I was hired two weeks ago."

"He never mentioned it to me."

The man's arrogance grated on Ty's nerves. "Not my concern." He pushed his chair back, nodded toward the irritated man and ambled out the door, certain he had not heard the last from Hank Walker.

CHAPTER
Three

Emma had the horse out of the stall and saddled in record time, so angry she was on the verge of tears. A hard tug on the cinch gave evidence of her indignation. "I swear, Midnight, if one more cowboy rides up and says he wants to marry me, I won't be responsible for what happens." She grabbed up the reins, loped out of the barn and turned west but stopped when hailed by one of the hands.

"Ever'thing all right, Miss Emma? Where you off to in such a hurry?"

"I'm fine, Leo, just taking Midnight for a quick ride."

"Ain't the new foreman gonna be here today?"

"I won't be gone long." Gentle pressure to the horse's flanks sent the mare into a gallop before Leo could say anything else. She had to get away before she exploded, or worse, broke down in front of the men.

Once out of sight, tears flowed freely, their salty trails

drying as Midnight's powerful legs ate up the ground. She reached the edge of Cherokee Creek three miles from the ranch and pulled to stop under the shade of a massive live oak. Her legs shook as she dismounted, sank to the ground, and cried until only soft hiccups remained.

Drained, she sat up and patted the nose pressed to her cheek. "How could he put me out there like a prized heifer for sale to the highest bidder?"

The horse snorted and nudged again.

"He put up posters, Midnight. Posters! All over the place. Even advertised in the Ft. Worth paper." Heat crept into her cheeks as she recalled the line of men, young and old, who had paraded through the house the last ten days, offering their services as a husband, among other things, which mortified her soul.

Hank Walker topped the list.

She still trembled at the thought. He made her uneasy, though she couldn't pinpoint the precise reason why. On the surface he appeared cordial and polite, and while not handsome, he wasn't bad. But a look appeared in his dull, brown eyes from time to time that made her skin crawl.

There were others after him, some shy and embarrassed, others blatantly masculine and overbearing who became angry when refused. Which explained the holstered Colt on her thigh. Whether coincidence or by design, one of her regular hands was always nearby when a new suitor came to call, and she appreciated their concern and show of support.

For her, marriage to anyone, especially those who called on her these days, meant the loss of the one thing she would never give up – her independence.

A life where she lacked the freedom to ride where and

when she pleased, work with the cattle, sleep under the stars, and work side-by-side with men who respected her as the boss was completely unimaginable. Her father wanted her to believe they only obeyed because he still lived, but she knew better. The road to respect and acceptance was hard and long, but she'd made it to the end, and would never give it up… even if it meant spending the rest of her life alone.

She loved her father, would do anything for him, but this was too much to ask. She simply didn't understand why he would force her to do something so repulsive. How could he expect her to marry someone she did not love; someone who didn't love her? Hell, some of these cowboys she had never even met before they showed up on her doorstep with professions of love and devotion.

They wanted the ranch. Not her, though he didn't seem to agree.

A lot of people in town laughed at her behind her back. She heard their snickers and snide remarks, but ignored them. She had only two friends, both of whom were married. Mable Barker at the general store, and Sally Owens from the Lazy O, with whom she had been friends since childhood.

Mable, older than Emma by ten years, and a mail order bride herself, quickly gave advice, solicited or not. "You wanna get a man, Emma, you gotta trade them britches for a skirt."

Emma insisted she did not want to get married and if she did, the man must accept her as she was, britches and all.

"A man don't want a woman who looks like a man. You're beautiful when you get gussied up. I don't see why you hide it."

She shook her head at the disquieting memories and lay

on the cool grass, enjoying the balmy spring breeze. Her lips curled up in soft smile as one last thought swept through before sleep overtook her - *I wonder if Grey Eyes needs a wife?*

Ty took a less direct route to the ranch arriving from the north to get a feel for the lay of the land. He reined Diablo to a stop near the top of a small rise and surveyed the awe-inspiring expanse of rolling green hills divided by the rushing waters of Cherokee Creek. His beautiful Eden's Garden plantation once overlooked such a vista. *Don't go there; Eden is gone.*

Most days the abysmal hole in his heart went unnoticed, the pain as much a part of him as an arm or leg, but every now and again, a reminder of life before that horrible war popped up; his family, his fiancé, and the pain rushed in anew, taking his breath away. He clenched his teeth and with much effort, pushed it back to the darkened corner of his mind where it belonged.

He nudged his mount into a slow walk while he studied the range he would soon be responsible for, at least temporarily. From what Henry said, it was a prized spread, and based on what he saw to this point, he agreed. Verdant pastures sprinkled with Longhorns and sturdy mustangs as far as the eye could see, dotted with massive oaks, pines and assorted Texas foliage. Cypress trees hugged the banks of the creek, which looked to be roughly twenty-feet wide, and patches of early wildflowers added vivid splashes of color. The creek disappeared behind another rise off to the left, and he headed toward it.

He stopped short when he saw her lying on the ground.

His thought at first she had fallen from her horse and might be hurt. Then she moved, stretched slightly, and he decided she was fast asleep. He dismounted and left Diablo back far enough not to disturb the woman or the horse, and walked forward, transfixed by the beauty in front of him.

Face turned toward the sun, one hand pillowed her head, the other rested on the grip of the Colt strapped to a shapely thigh. Although dressed in jeans and a man's shirt, a woman's body was easily discernable. His quickly noted long legs and well-rounded hips, moving up to a narrow waist, then to full breasts that strained against the buttons of the too-tight shirt. Chestnut hair caught with streaks of golden fire fanned out around her head like a bonnet. Sun-kissed complexion, delicately arched brows, and full lips, edges tilted up in a serene smile that made him wonder what she dreamed, completed the package before him.

If this woman is Emma Marshall, this foreman job just got a lot more interesting.

He considered waking her but discarded the notion. Certain the dirty smudges on her cheeks resulted from dried tears, he decided whatever she did here was personal and private, and he would not interrupt.

But that smile…what dream put it there?

She stretched out one leg and arched her back like a cat. Unwanted visions of those long legs wrapped around his waist blindsided him. He tried to look away but his gaze hit the top button of her shirt, dangerously close to popping open, and the effect hit him hard and fast. Before he did something really stupid, he spun around, and walked back to his horse.

He led the animal some distance away, then mounted, and headed for the ranch, vision clouded by a single button.

It was the very best dream ever, no doubt about it. She didn't need to see his cool, grey eyes to know it was him atop a glorious stallion. He smiled, slow and sexy as he dismounted and walked toward her, his voice a deep, raspy whisper when he called her name.

Miss me, Em?

The tingle in the pit of her stomach became a throb and she arched toward him. You know I have.

Are you happy to see me?

Come here and I'll show you.

He knelt down beside her and leaned over, his lips –

Midnight snorted and startled her awake.

She covered her eyes with her arm and groaned. "Aww, Midnight, why now?" She sat up and hugged her bent knees. A glance at the sun told her she'd been gone longer than she intended, but still she lingered.

This was her favorite place on the ranch; peaceful and secluded yet close enough it would be easy to get back fast, which she needed to do.

Icy water from the creek removed the smudges from her face, chased away the remnants of sleep, and the troubling dream. A crumpled red bandana pulled from the pocket of tight-fighting jeans, held the unruly curls together at the nape of her neck. She mounted Midnight and headed back to the ranch at a gallop.

"Aw hell," she moaned upon seeing four horses tied to the rail in front of the house, Hank Walker's big sorrel among them.

"Dammit!" Midnight's ears twitched at the harsh

expletive. "This day just keeps gettin' better."

Leo waited at the landing. "Miss Emma." He touched the brim of his hat. "I'll take care of Midnight for you since you got more company."

"Thank you, Leo."

"Mr. Walker got here 'bout the time the other fellers did and he took 'em inside like he owned the place." His pinched expression reflected dislike for Walker. He took Midnight's reins and headed for the barn. "I'll be around if you need anything, ma'am."

A quick inhale brought with it the scent of fresh cut pine mixed with her mother's roses and immediately revived her flagging spirit. Voices sent her down the hall to the office on the right. She stopped when she entered, hands fisted at her side when she saw Hank Walker sitting at the desk, two cowboys standing in front.

"Just so we are clear," Walker pulled a cigar from his pocket and sniffed it. "If you are here about the posters, you can leave now. That situation has been handled."

Situation? Handled?

Two long strides put her beside the desk. "What the hell are you doing?" Her sharp question was aimed at Walker but the force in her voice had the two cowhands stepping back. Walker's lips curled into an indulgent smile.

Her temper shot up several degrees.

"I was merely telling these young men you are no longer in the market for a husband."

"And what gave you that right, Mr. Walker?"

He rounded the desk, reached for her hands. "Emma, you need to stop this and marry me like your father wants."

Instinct urged her to step back, but she stood fast, hands

out of his reach. "And what about what I want?

His smile turned malicious. "A man knows what is best for his woman."

His woman?

She teetered on the edge of an explosive reaction. *How dare he!*

The audience—and her immense control—were the only two things keeping her from telling him exactly where he could go. Her heart raced, fists clenched so tight nails bit into her palms. "Mr. Walker—"

"Emma…I thought we were past such formalities." He reached for her hands again.

His patronizing tone sent her anger up another notch and she silently counted to ten. "I am Miss Marshall to you." She faced him, back straight, shoulders squared and easily met his gaze since he stood only a few inches over her own five-foot-nine frame. "I've tried to be considerate, and spare your feelings. Obviously, I wasted my time. So let me be perfectly clear." She spoke each word precisely. "I will not marry you under *any* circumstances."

"Emma – "

"I think the lady made her position pretty plain."

She whirled toward the voice and her heart all but stopped before it kicked into a stampede.

She couldn't breathe. She couldn't look away.

It was him. The man who haunted her dreams. Right there in front of her.

CHAPTER
Four

Ty watched the exchange between the woman and Walker with interest. He disliked the man on sight. His aversion increased when he assumed the position of person in charge as soon as he arrived, ushering them inside before sitting at the desk like king of the hill. Since he had no idea what kind of control the man actually wielded, he waited.

Now he knew.

Four sets of eyes watched with varying degrees of interest and dislike as Ty stepped away from the corner from which he watched the room. He kept his attention on Walker but a quick glance at Miss Marshall made him think she just saw a ghost.

"Now, see here, Tyler, this is none of your concern."

"Like I said, she's Mr. Marshall's daughter, which makes her my concern."

"Stop talking about me like I'm not in the room!"

Her angry retort had everyone looking at her.

Ty touched the brim of his hat. "My apologies, Miss Marshall. I meant no disrespect. I'm Tyler Roundtree, the new foreman." He nodded toward Walker. "He looked to be in charge when I got here. I can see now that is not the case."

She looked at him a moment and appeared to have trouble breathing. Her chest rose and fell like she were gasping for air. Without a word, she sat down in the chair vacated by Walker, hands clasped in front. "I'm in charge here. Mr. Walker has no authority over anything." She cut those flashing emerald orbs toward Walker. "Or anyone."

She inhaled deeply and looked at Ty. "I'm sorry I wasn't here when you arrived."

"No problém, ma'am. I'm sure you have a lot to handle these days." *Damn. No wonder you were off crying by yourself.*

Her cheeks turned a rosy shade of pink as she looked away from him to the two cowboys who still stood in front of the desk, nervously rolling their hat brims. "Wally Kincaid and Jake Walton isn't it?"

"Yes, ma'am," replied the one nearest Ty. "Jake and me ain't here 'bout them posters. I mean, we would, you know, if you…well, we…" His face flamed all the way up to his hairline. "What I mean is, we wanted to know if you needed us for the round-up again this spring."

"Of course. You're excellent hands." She glanced at Ty never quite meeting his eyes and quickly looked away. "These men have assisted with the roundup the last couple of years. You got any questions for them?"

"No, ma'am. I understand you've been running things for a while so I reckon you know what you need."

Walker didn't give up. "Emma, you really should let Tyler

handle this. I'm sure there are other things for a woman to take care of."

She sat up straighter. The look she gave Walker could've melted steel and Ty's admiration for her grit shot up several notches.

And she was the most wildly beautiful creature he had ever seen.

"There are no legal matters for you to attend to, Mr. Walker, therefore, you may leave now."

He opened his mouth and shut it when she continued.

"And do not *ever* presume to answer for me or make decisions for me again. You are my family's attorney. Nothing more. Good day, sir."

Walker's face glowed bright red and his eyes spit fire as he looked at Ty who glared right back.

With one final look at Emma, who ignored him, the disgruntled attorney grabbed the black felt derby from the corner of the desk and slapped it on his head. He never looked back as he stomped from the room.

Emma shuffled papers around and her voice shook as she spoke to cowhands. "Looks like we'll start in a couple of weeks, probably around the fifteenth or so. Work for you?"

"Yes, ma'am," replied the men in unison.

"Good. Find Mr. Roundtree here a few of days before to make sure nothing has changed."

"Yes, ma'am, Miss Emma," said Wally who evidently acted as unofficial spokesman for the pair. "We'll be here."

Once alone, she had trouble meeting his gaze and shuffled the papers again.

Ty's attention kept drifting to that damn button and he had to work to keep from staring at it.

"I'm sorry I wasn't here when you arrived, Mr. Roundtree, I –"

"I go by Tyler or Ty, if you don't mind, Miss Marshall, and I only arrived a few minutes ago. In fact, me and those two hands arrived about the same time. Walker was already here."

She jerked her head up and looked at him. "Here? In my office?"

He shook his head. "On the porch. I actually met him in town this morning. It didn't appear he knew the other two, just assumed he knew why they were here."

The blush deepened and those compelling green pools met his squarely. "I'm sure you've seen or heard about the posters and the ad my father is responsible for."

"Yes ma'am. But don't see it has anything to do with my job."

Anger, stark and vivid glittered in her eyes, resonated in her voice. "I heard you tell Mr. Walker I was your concern when I walked in."

Yep. Prickly as a cactus. "Way I see it, you're the boss while your Pa is sick. Part of my job is watching out for the boss."

She bristled. "I can take care of myself."

"Yes ma'am, I reckon you can. But even the best of us need someone to watch our backs." He nodded toward the window where he watched Walker mount his horse. "A man like him don't take to bein' bested…especially by a woman."

She chewed her lower lip then seemed to accept his response.

"I've worked beside my father since I was ten years old. And I've run this place alone while he's been sick. I work alongside my men and don't expect, or ask for, special con-siderations." She rounded the desk. "You got a problem with taking orders from a woman?"

"Not as long as she knows what she's doing." He paused a moment. "And from what I hear, you do."

Her brow furrowed slightly as though questioning what he said.

Obviously not accustomed to compliments, even light ones.

"My father asked to speak with you as soon as you ar-rived." She headed for the door. "I'll take you to him now and we can tour the ranch and meet the others later."

She didn't look back to see if he followed as she headed up the stairs to her father's room.

Whoever said women shouldn't wear pants never saw Emma Marshall in a pair.

CHAPTER
Five

EMMA KEPT HER GAZE ON THE STAIRS AND TRIED NOT TO think about the new foreman a step behind her or how his sudden appearance left her shaken. Her initial shock was quickly replaced by a shiver of awareness so unexpected, her breath caught.

Mr. Grey Eyes is here.

His voice, while not the raspy whisper of her dream lover, was nonetheless a deep, throaty sound that made her stomach quiver. A southern accent, not Texas, but definitely the south made it quite pleasant to listen to.

An imposing figure, he stood at least six-four, with broad shoulders and thick, muscular thighs. His face was all sharp angles and planes, deeply tanned and covered with dense beard stubble. Stormy gray eyes she remembered so well were fringed with long lashes and rested beneath thick, dark brows. A jagged scar ran up his left cheekbone to the edge of an inky-black hairline. Full lips rested below a Roman nose with a slight crook to it.

He was the most handsome man she had ever seen in her life.

And her new foreman.

She would be working with him. Closely. Every day. She sighed and opened the door to her father's room.

"Pa, this is Mr. Roundtree – Tyler. The new foreman Henry sent over."

Ty shook hands with her father. "Pleased to meet you, Mr. Marshall."

"Likewise young man. Thank you for agreeing to – " A fit of coughing left him gasping for air and ended whatever he planned to say next.

Emma sat on the edge of the bed waiting for the spell to pass, her stomach in knots, hands fisted in her lap. When it passed, she filled a glass with water from the pitcher on the bedside table and offered it to him, unable to hide the tremble that caused the glass to shake as he drank.

He took a few sips and shook his head. "No more," he whispered as he lay back down.

She set the glass down and struggled to speak, but nothing got past the lump in her throat. *He leaves me a little more every day. How much longer can he hold on? What ever will I do without him?* She had to blink several times in an effort to stop the ocean of tears banked inside.

The gentle pressure of Tyler's hand on her shoulder in silent support, startled her. Under different circumstances she would have shaken off such a display and berated the person foolish enough to think she needed it. But for some reason, his touch soothed her, its warmth thawed the icy blood running through her veins, and the trembles eased.

"Emma Rose?"

She started when he called her by her full name since he rarely called her anything but *girl*. Recovering quickly, she took his hand and squeezed, shocked at its lack of warmth. "I'm here, Papa. I'm here."

He didn't say anything more for several heartbeats which scared her more than she would admit.

He gave her a weak smile. "I ain't gone yet."

She swallowed twice before she spoke, glad her voice didn't betray her concern. "I can see that."

He gave her a small smile, his gaze moving to the hand resting on her shoulder. He stared at it hand a moment then closed his eyes again. "I'm right tired, Emma-Girl. Why don't you show him around? I'll see you at supper."

She sat there until the steady rise and fall of his chest confirmed he slept.

"How bad is it?"

Tyler's soft-spoken question broke through the fog of despair threatening to engulf her.

She adjusted the quilt around the sleeping man. "Bad enough."

She didn't realize Tyler's hand still rested on her shoulder until she stood and it dropped away leaving her longing for its warmth again. "Let's go down to the kitchen. I'm sure lunch is ready now. Afterwards, I'll introduce you to the hands and we can take a tour of the ranch."

"Sounds good."

Her cottony mouth made speaking difficult, but limiting the conversation to inconsequential things made it easier. "Any questions come to mind as we go along, just ask."

"I will."

The afternoon passed quickly. The men, guarded at first, soon warmed to him after hearing Henry Owens recommended him, which pleased Emma a lot. Ole Pete had been the foreman here since before her mother died and filling his shoes would be difficult.

And though she would never admit it to anyone, she liked him immediately, which shocked her. He possessed an easy-going manner that made talking effortless and she caught herself several times before sharing too much.

The intense physical attraction was something else altogether.

Never had she experienced such a reaction before and was totally unprepared for the quickened pace of her heart or difficulty just getting enough air in her lungs. And the unfamiliar warmth coursing through her veins caused her anxiety to escalate. Uncharted territory for her, this required careful navigation.

Right now, the swarm of butterflies residing in her stomach threatened to take flight at any moment, adding to an already explosive anxiety level.

He doesn't remember meeting you. He's only here until we find someone permanent. Don't go getting any ideas about him.

She had a sinking suspicion it was already too late for those warnings.

CHAPTER
Six

THE SUN HOVERED JUST ABOVE THE TREE LINE, TURNING the sky a brilliant blend of purple, blue and orange while the air carried the pungent aroma of cattle, sage and something Emma secretly called the scent of Ty.

He sat with his hands crossed on the pommel of his saddle gazing at the panorama before them as they took a break under the oak by the creek. They had ridden the range for several hours today marking where the cattle they would be rounding up in a few days grazed, yet he didn't seem tired at all.

In the three weeks since he came to Twin Oaks, Ty captivated Emma's thoughts as she tried to make sense of what happened to her anytime they were together.

The shiver running through her now had nothing to do with the slight chill that still lingered in the air after sundown.

"This is the prettiest spot on the ranch." Emma hoped

her voice didn't sound as strange to him as it did to her.

"Yeah, thought so, too, first time I saw it."

Emma didn't think they had been here since he arrived. "You've been here before? When?"

She wasn't certain in the failing light, but got the distinct impression he blushed. He definitely seemed nervous as he fidgeted in the saddle and avoided looking at her.

He ducked his head and nodded. "I came by here on my way from town when I first arrived. Just wanted to look things over. Didn't think you'd mind."

She hooked her right leg over the saddle horn, completely at ease on her horse. "Of course not."

Ty nodded to the hill just off to the right. "That would be a great spot for a house. Plenty of trees for shade and….what a view."

Does he read minds, too? A soft "Yes it would," was all she managed to say. Her dream of a home of her own here one day would most likely die with her father.

She gave herself a quick mental shake to erase the depressing thought, and leaned back, resting both hands behind the saddle. "I love this place. The flowers, the trees, even the water has a pleasant smell."

"It's a right pretty sight for sure."

She glanced his way and found him watching her. Unfamiliar longing whispered through her, settled low in her belly, its ache making her squirm. "Why do you call him Diablo? The name doesn't seem to fit him."

He smiled and her gut clenched. He was, without a doubt, the handsomest man she'd ever seen, scar and all. In fact, it made him more attractive. Even with her above-average height, she felt small and delicate around him, and for the first time in her life, found herself wishing she understood how to be the kind of woman who would interest someone like him. She looked away before he read those thoughts in her face.

"Most times he's fine. Sometimes though, he just goes nuts. Never know what will set him off. Left me sitting in the middle of a river once. Had to walk two miles to find him."

As if on cue, Diablo chose that moment to go nuts.

He reared up on his hind legs, pawing the air, and let loose a shrill whinny. When his hooves hit the ground, he pranced, snorted and bucked as Ty tugged on the reins, cussing a blue streak trying to get him under control.

The unexpected activity startled Midnight who shied away so quickly, Emma had no time to react. In a heartbeat, she lay on her back on the ground, while her ride bolted off toward the ranch.

When she hit the ground, Ty nearly lost it. He jerked hard on the reins to get Diablo under control, never thinking about the words coming out of his mouth. "Are you hurt?" he yelled as he fought his mount.

She sat up but didn't stand. "I'm fine. Just embarrassed I got tossed." She twisted around and watched Midnight race away, then fixed him with leaf green eyes laced with humor. "Now I see why you call him Diablo."

The devil horse suddenly stopped prancing and stood there blowing hard. "I can't get off or we'll both be walking. Do you need a hand to get up?" He leaned toward her and extended his hand.

She shook her head. "No, I'm good. Nothin' hurt but my pride." With a grunt, she stood and brushed dirt from her backside before turning to face him, hands on her hips. "What on earth set him off?"

"Who the hell knows?" He didn't bother to hide his disgust.

She laughed, a soft musical sound with the power to send desire coursing through him.

"Why do you keep him?"

One corner of his mouth kicked up. "Glutton for punishment, I guess."

Her smile overpowered him and Ty's heart rate jumped. Something about her triggered every male cell in his body, and it scared the hell out of him. He'd been in love once in his life and the war took that away, too.

He would not risk his heart again.

But damned if he didn't enjoy just being around her, especially when those defensive walls she fought so hard to keep in place dropped a little. She wavered between brash and bold or timid and shy. All business when the crew was around but during those times they were alone, he caught brief glimpses of the woman behind the man's clothes and his body begged for more.

Dammit. Thoughts like that are a waste of time. She's off limits.

He bent forward, hand extended. "Come on, you'll have to ride in front."

"What?"

Her startled expression and the pink tinge easing up her cheeks delighted him. "Behind will be too close to his flanks and we might both end up walking."

She looked at the pommel, him and back. "You want me to ride in front of you?"

"Yep."

"Are you sure he can handle both of us? I might be too heavy."

He grinned. *You're just right.* "Trust me. You're not too heavy."

Her face glowed scarlet and she avoided meeting his eyes. *Damned if she isn't the prettiest thing I've ever seen.*

"I can walk. It's only a mile or two."

"It's a good three miles and you're not walking." He took his boot out the stirrup. "Give me your hand."

He expected her to refuse and mentally prepared – looked forward – to arguing with her about it. Instead, she squared her shoulders and stepped forward.

He got her seated sideways in front of him, right leg hooked over the pommel, like riding side-saddle, and immediately regretted it. The proximity of her body to his sent lightning bolts of awareness through him. Her hip nestled against his groin and unless he concentrated on something like dead horses and war-torn limbs, she would soon know what a scoundrel she had working for her.

This is going to be the longest three miles of my life.

CHAPTER
Seven

EMMA STRUGGLED FOR AIR AND HER HEART RATE accelerated to the point of dizziness. A steadying inhalation inundated her with the musky smell of man, horse and leather which quickly made bad matters worse.

She gripped Diablo's mane for balance, and tried to keep from touching any more of Ty than necessary, which proved to be an exercise in futility. His arms circled her waist, one leg rested over his thigh and she realized it wasn't his belt buckle pressing against her hip.

"I'm going to keep him at a walk for a spell. He's usually worn out after these episodes."

Ty's breath, warm against her cheek, produced immediate tingles of awareness coursing through her. Her voice refused to cooperate, so she nodded.

"I'm sorry for my language back there when I was wrestling with my horse. That's no way to talk in front of a lady."

She snorted. "I've been called a lot of things, but don't think *lady* is one of them."

"You are to me."

For whatever reason, his remark pleased her immensely.

Ty nudged the horse forward with gentle pressure from his knees that transmitted through the leg resting on his thigh, sending those damn butterflies into another rampage.

Emma didn't consider herself naïve. Inexperienced, yes, but not naïve. She grew up on a ranch, after all, and while she never personally experienced the man-woman thing, she comprehended the gist of what happened, thanks to enlightening conversations with her two best friends.

At least, she thought she did.

Determined to dismiss the strange new sensations overwhelming her, she tried again for normal conversation. "How often does this happen?" *Could I possibly sound any more nervous?*

He shrugged. "Not often, but enough to keep me on my toes."

She struggled to speak coherently as the warmth and scent of him wormed its way to her core. "What causes it?"

"No idea. The bast – the man I bought him from treated him poorly. Maybe he has some kind of brain damage." Ty grunted. "Or maybe he really *is* a devil horse."

She giggled, then turned sober. "I hate people who mistreat animals. And kids, too."

"Yeah, they're a sorry lot."

She sat at an awkward angle, trying not to lean against him, and soon suffered a cramp in her back and she shifted to ease the pain.

"You all right?"

His mouth brushed her ear, and gooseflesh erupted on her arms. "A little cramp in my back."

He pulled on the reins, and Diablo obediently stopped. "No wonder. You're stiff as a board. Swing your leg over the pommel and sit in front of me. You'll be more comfortable."

He didn't give her time to reply. Instead, he took her shoulders and turned her slightly where her back rested against his chest. "You don't have to keep your knee like that; you can swing it over."

The husky timbre in his voice made her stomach tighten and it took two attempts to answer. "I'm good."

Gentle pressure from his knees and the horse resumed its leisurely pace.

She tried in vain to come up with a topic of conversation to distract her thoughts from the warm, broad chest at her back. She swallowed hard as heat curled down her spine and unfamiliar desire flared.

"He doesn't seem to be getting any better."

She intuitively understood he referred to her father. "He's dying." She said the words without emotion despite the pain ripping through her.

He remained silent a moment. "I'm sorry."

She bit her lower lip for control. "Thanks."

Ty exhaled and the air tickled her ear, causing her whole body to quiver.

"Ummm…that explains why he wants you married."

She tried to glance at him over her shoulder but all she could see were his lips which almost touched her nose. She looked forward again. "Why do you say that?

One shoulder lifted slightly. "It's what I'd do."

"Why?"

He shrugged again. "You're an only child."

"So?"

"Do you have other family?"

"An uncle near Ft. Worth. A couple of older cousins."

He shrugged as though she just answered the question.

"I still don't understand."

Ty looked at her a long moment before replying and the butterflies dipped lower, scattering like a covey of quail, triggering an involuntary shiver she covered by facing forward again.

"He wants to make sure you are taken care of when he's gone."

She stiffened. "I can take care of myself."

"That's not what I meant." He pulled the horse to a stop again, hands all but resting in her lap.

Definitely not his belt buckle.

It took supreme effort on her part but she turned and looked him in the eye and didn't swoon. "Then what?"

He stared off as though gathering his thoughts, then faced her, expression unreadable. "You are his only daughter. He is dying. He doesn't want you to be alone."

She snorted and faced forward again. "He wants a man to run Twin Oaks because he doesn't think a woman can."

He shook his head and nudged his mount forward. "Stubborn woman."

His statement stuck in her mind. Surely that wasn't the reason for her father's ultimatum? Was it? Her brain dashed from one what-if to another, and despair weighed her down. She bit her lip and fought back tears. *How much longer will he be here? How can I go on without him? Oh God… I'm so tired. What I wouldn't give for a decent night's sleep.*

The rhythmic sway of the horse's movements coupled with the comforting warmth radiating from Ty soothed her to the point the disquieting thoughts slowly drifted away and she did the unthinkable…fell fast asleep nestled in the arms of her dream lover.

Ty's attraction to Emma stymied him. Had he ever been this attracted to someone he just met? *Jennie…it was that way with Jennie.* Sweet, delicate Jennie whose refined beauty captured him from the beginning.

She and Emma were opposites in every way. Jennie, with her ivory skin and corn silk hair was a lady born of wealth and privilege. Quiet and dutiful, she personified grace and elegance. Emma was all fire and passion, with enough determination to tackle anything, whose burnished curls and emerald eyes made him long for things he could never have.

I like her grit. Nothing more.

Her father's illness took its toll, though. She threw herself into every chore, every task, defensive walls firmly in place, pushing herself to exhaustion. *You work so you won't think… I know.*

Smiles were rare, but the transformation amazing. Ty would do anything to make her smile. Even tussle with the devil horse.

The fact that she fell asleep so quickly testified to her level of fatigue. He kept the horse to a sedate walk, both because he didn't want to push the unpredictable stallion and because Emma needed the rest, no matter how short the duration. And he enjoyed having her in his arms, head lolled back on his shoulder, even breathing punctuated by an occasional light snore indicating how deeply she slept. He smiled. *She'd have a conniption fit if I told her she snored.*

Suddenly, a soft whimper seeped from her throat, and her head rolled from side to side.

"Shhh, Em…shhh, it's all right…rest easy." He tightened his arm around her waist. "No bad dreams allowed," Ty murmured as though talking to a skittish horse, not really thinking about what he said, just the tone of his voice.

Soon, she relaxed, rested her temple against his cheek and exhaled.

All his protective instincts, and something more primal he chose not to dwell on, sprang to life. *She's alone with no one to look out for her.*

Despite her statements to the contrary, she needed someone to help her.

She needed him.

He jerked in the saddle causing Diablo to snort and shy sideways. He relaxed and pulled gently on the reins. "Easy boy, easy. Didn't mean to scare you."

She needs me.

CHAPTER
Eight

HALF A MILE FROM THE RANCH, A CLOUD OF DUST IN THE distance alerted Ty to expect company soon. *I guess Midnight made it home.* He looked at the head still nestled against cheek, reluctant to wake her. *She'd be embarrassed if the men saw her…and pissed at me, no doubt.* One side of his mouth curled up. She was a sight to behold when riled.

He nudged her arm. "Emma…wake up. Almost home." *Home.* When had Twin Oaks become *home*?

She murmured something unintelligible, and snuggled closer.

Desired blazed to life and his body throbbed. "Damn," he whispered. "Come on, Em, wake up. Riders coming."

She sighed and pressed against his chest.

He gritted his teeth. "Em…dammit, Em, wake up. Riders coming.'"

She breathed in and slowly opened her eyes…then jerked

back like she had been shot. Diablo sidestepped quickly forcing her to grab his arm for balance.

"Enjoy your nap?" Ty kept his voice calm revealing nothing of the chaos her proximity caused him. Mostly.

She shifted on his lap, hand still gripping his arm, and he stifled a groan. "Stop twitching."

"How long did I sleep?"

Her voice, raspy with sleep, caused his body to sizzle.

"Not long. An hour maybe."

"An hour!" Her head darted toward the approaching riders. "Why didn't you wake me before now?"

"If you didn't need the sleep, you would've been awake for the ride."

The arriving search party ended any retort she considered.

"Miss Emma," said Leo, concern etching lines on his face, eyes darting to the hand clutching Ty's arm, "you all right?"

"I'm fine, Leo."

Henry held Midnight's reins. "What happened?"

Ty noted the bright flush creeping up her cheeks but she didn't duck her head when she replied.

"Diablo…"

Henry started laughing. "What'd he do this time?"

Ty didn't miss the fact she still held on to his arm and hadn't yet attempted to get off his lap.

Neither did Leo. His pained expression said it all.

He's in love with her.

"Fine one minute, nuts the next. Startled her horse."

Emma snorted. "She tossed me like a damned greenhorn and took off."

Henry was the only one who smiled.

"I…we was worried when Midnight come in without you. Are you sure you're okay? Can you ride?"

Ty kept his expression neutral.

She tensed as though just remembering where she sat and quickly released his shirt. "Um, yes, I'm fine. Probably sore tomorrow, though."

Ty placed a hand on her arm when she started to move. "Hang on." He dismounted, wrapped his hands around her waist, and placed her on the ground.

And she let him.

So what if he kept his hands on her a waist a fraction longer than required? He just wanted to make sure she was able stand on her own. If Leo happened to see and got the wrong idea…*What the hell am I doing?*

She reached for Midnight's reins and mounted. "Is Sarah at the house, Henry?"

"Yep. Insisted I come along to make sure you were okay." He looked at Ty and grinned. "Told her you were in good hands."

She nodded and set off at a trot, the rest of the group falling in line.

Henry rode beside Ty. "Anything you wanna talk about?"

"Like what?"

He shrugged. "You and Emma seem to be gettin' on pretty good." He shook his head and grinned. "There ain't a man around who could've gotten her to ride in front of him *and* help her down like you just did. Not even Leo."

"She know how he feels?"

"Saw that, did you?"

"Hard to miss."

Henry looked straight ahead. "Emma's special to us. I'd

hate to see her get hurt."

Ty tugged on the reins, stopping his horse. "You wanna spell it out and quit beatin' 'round the bush."

"You told me yourself; you ain't the settlin' down type. I just don't want her hurt when you go."

"She won't be." He kneed Diablo and took off at a gallop leaving Henry to follow.

Emma's cheeks burned. *I fell asleep in his lap!* She tried to ignore how her hand still tingled from contact with his chest.

Leo followed as she dismounted in front of the house, while the others left to complete their assigned tasks. "I'll take care of Midnight, ma'am."

"That won't be necessary, Leo, thank you. Only one more section to look over before dark. I won't be here long."

As she spoke, Ty and Henry rode up. It took all her grit to face him and not flinch, unable to stop or hide the rush of heat to her cheeks. "I'd like to say hello to Sarah and then we can finish what we started." Even to her, the statement sounded intimate.

One corner of his mouth curled up and the bottom dropped out of her stomach.

"Ready when you are."

Henry spoke up. "I know you and Sarah have a lot of catching up do. Ty and me can check it out. Where did you leave off?"

Henry's face revealed nothing of his thoughts as she told them where to look then turned for the door. "Supper will be at seven. See you both then."

She rushed inside before passing out from embarrassment. *He saw me in Ty's lap! So did Leo!*

Though not experienced with the opposite sex, she wasn't blind to the fact Leo appeared sweet on her and she did her best not to encourage it. She liked him, of course, he worked hard and he a nice person to boot. But he didn't make her heart stutter or leave her excited and off-balance like Ty did with just a look.

"Are you all right?" Sarah's hug was hampered by the girth of her pregnancy. "I was so worried when your horse came in without you."

"I'm fine. Not the first time I've been tossed."

"What on earth happened?"

Sarah listened intently as they walked to the office and sat on the small couch.

"So…how was it?" Sarah's bright blue eyes sparkled and her honey gold curls bobbed as she shifted on the seat.

Confused by the question, Emma looked at her friend and blinked. "What? Getting tossed?"

"No, silly. Riding in his lap. What was it like?"

Emma looked away quickly—too quickly, and stammered. "I don't know, fine I guess." *I would gladly get tossed again to be held like that.*

"Fine?" Sarah grabbed her arm. "You guess?"

Emma huffed and looked toward the window. "If you must know, I slept most of the way."

Sarah's mouth gaped open. "You rode in his lap? And *slept*?"

"Not exactly *in* his lap. More like across it…sort of like side-saddle." She shrugged. "And I was tired." *He's so warm and strong.*

Sarah beamed. "But you enjoyed it, right? Having his arms around you while you slept?"

Emma's face burned. She'd cut out her tongue before she admitted to anyone just how much she did like it. "Well, it wasn't awful."

Sarah paused. "I've known you since we were ten years old and I've never, ever seen you blush."

Her hushed statement brought a new surge of color to Emma's cheeks and she went to the desk, shuffling papers without seeing them.

"You like him, don't you?"

"Of course. He's a good foreman. I'm glad Henry sent him over."

"That's not what I mean and you know it." Sarah didn't let up. "You like him. As a woman likes a man."

She flinched. Sarah's observation was way too close to the truth. "No! Are you crazy?"

"I think he's just what you need."

"What?" Emma's heart rate escalated and she gasped. "No!"

"Why not? You need a husband, Ty needs a wife."

Emma sat at the desk, pulling open the top ledger. "You're out of your mind. No way in hell would someone like him be interested in someone like me."

"Who are you trying to convince, Emma?" She paused. "Henry said Ty has been…adrift since the war ended. Lost everything; his home, his whole family, his fiancée. He's wandered from place to place with no roots, no reason to stay anywhere for long. Henry and me are about his only family."

Emma glared. "Is there a point in there somewhere?"

"You grinned when you glanced back and saw him riding

in behind you. You hid it fast, but I saw it."

"I smiled. So what. Everybody smiles."

"You don't."

"Sarah, I –"

"And I saw the way he looked at your backside when you stepped up on the porch."

Emma stared at the ledger without seeing it, pulse pounding so hard she saw spots in her eyes.

Sarah rubbed her swollen belly and smirked. "I know desire when I see it."

Emma jerked upright. "What? No! You must be mistaken."

"Why is it so hard for you to see what a stunning woman you are?"

"Because I'm not blind! I'm not beautiful like you or even Mable. I'm too tall, my hair is a mess. I have no…no feminine wiles. And even if I did, I wouldn't know what to do with them."

"Do you want to?"

Emma stared, not comprehending this change in conversation. "Want to what?"

"Know what to do with your feminine wiles?" Her smile grew wider. "Because I can teach you."

CHAPTER
Nine

Ty stood back as Henry greeted Rafe Marshall. Their warm smiles and firm handshakes indicated both men held tremendous respect for each other. *I once had that kind of respect.* He pushed the troubling thought away. *Can't live in the past. Get on with the present.*

"Thank you again for recommending Ty there, Henry. Damn good man."

Henry smiled at his friend. "You won't find a better one."

The compliments, unexpected and sincere, caught Ty off guard. "Thank you," he said softly.

"Not many men I know can deal with my Emma every day." Rafe's hoarse laugh was weak. "But you seem to do it just fine."

"She's a smart girl."

He grunted. "I wouldn't call her *girl* to her face."

"Not if you want to keep all your body parts intact," said Henry.

Ty shrugged. What could he say to that?

Rafe nodded toward the window which provided a view of the front yard, corrals and a corner of the barn. "I appreciate you suggesting we move my bed down from upstairs, Ty. I like bein' able to see what's going on outside."

He debated whether or not to tell him Emma suggested it and wanted him to get the credit because she didn't think Rafe would do it otherwise. Honesty won out. "Actually, it was Emma's idea. I just helped with the move."

Emma's father didn't speak for a heartbeat. "I was worried sick when Midnight come in without her. Henry assured me whatever happened, you would take care of Emma."

Ty quickly explained what happened.

Rafe's rusty laugh brought a touch of color to his ashen cheeks. "How'd you get her to do it? Hogtie her?"

Ty shook his head. "Told her she wasn't walking. Like I said, she's a smart girl – uh, woman, and knew I was right."

Rafe looked at Henry, then back to Ty. His left brow shot up and his lips twitched.

Ty eyed the two men staring at him with a combination of awe and amusement. *What the hell? She rode in front of me...what's the big deal?* "She's not unreasonable."

Rafe cackled. "Just wait, boy, just wait."

Further comments were halted by a quick knock on the door, and Sarah came wobbling in.

"Good evening, Mr. Rafe. You're looking much better today." She sat on the edge of the bed and patted his hand. "Emma wanted me to see if maybe you felt up to joining us for supper tonight instead of eating in here alone."

Rafe shook his head. "You young folks got a lot of catching up to do. Don't need an ol' fool like me in there."

"Nonsense," sniffed Sarah. "If you feel up to it, we insist you join us. I know Emma would be pleased."

Ty didn't think Rafe possessed the energy for it. His strength ebbed and flowed these days, but the smile on the older man's face at her suggestion made him swallow his concerns. Besides, he did think Emma would like having him there.

Henry helped get him in the rolling chair and Ty pushed him to the dining room.

Lupe added the last items to the center of the table when they entered. "*Señor* Rafe! So good to see you up." The cook pulled a chair from the head of the table. "He will sit here."

"Thank you, Lupe." Rafe smiled as he took his place at the head of the table.

Ty noted he already slumped a little in his chair and hoped the evening didn't do more harm than good.

"I don't know why they insisted I join 'em," Rafe declared. "Not much appetite these days."

"But you will be with your family, Señor Rafe, and that is more important."

Rafe looked around. "Where's Emma?"

Sarah and Lupe exchanged nervous looks. "She's getting ready," said Sarah, moving to the other side of the table to sit beside Henry. "She'll be along shortly."

"Gettin' ready?" Rafe's brows pulled together when he scowled.

Ty couldn't imagine what *getting ready* meant for Emma. He rarely saw her in anything but jeans and what he suspected to be her father's old shirts. A couple of Sundays back, she took the buggy to church and from a distance, it appeared she wore a dress, but he wasn't sure and never saw her return.

Thanks to Diablo, though, he experienced the softness of her skin and knew her hair held a faint fragrance of flowers, and her body possessed soft curves he ached to touch again.

"Something wrong, Ty?"

Henry's question pulled him from the snaky path he trod. "What?"

"You didn't answer Rafe's question."

He gave himself a hard, mental kick. *What the hell?* "I'm sorry, Mr. Marshall. Guess I was wool gathering. What did you ask?"

"Call me Rafe. How many head do you think – "

When he cut his comment short, Ty followed his surprised gaze and saw Emma standing in the doorway.

In a dress.

His mouth went dry. Latent desire simmering for weeks jumped to a rapid boil that took all his control to tamp down. *She's beautiful as a Texas sunset.*

Dark brown curls pulled up from the sides and secured by ivory combs exposed flushed, sun-kissed skin, while coffee-colored waves flowed over one shoulder and down her back. Her gown, a simple moss-green muslin with a square neckline, trimmed in white lace accentuated her full bust and fell in soft folds around her ankles. A darker green ribbon, tied in a neat bow on the side highlighted a small waist.

Anxious emerald eyes scanned the room, briefly met his, and darted away. She glided, graceful as any Atlanta belle, toward her father. "You act like you've never seen me in a dress, Papa." She gave him a quick kiss, then nervously patted his shoulder. "I'm so glad you felt up to joining us tonight."

He stared and swallowed hard. "Emma…you…you are as beautiful as your mother."

★ ★ ★

Of all the things Emma thought her father might say upon seeing her in something other than jeans and his old shirt, *that* wasn't one of them. She avoided looking at Ty as pleasure and embarrassment washed over her. "Thank you, Papa, though I think you exaggerate a bit."

"No. I don't."

"Green is definitely your color," added Henry.

"Isn't she lovely, Ty?"

Sarah's question caused Emma's nervousness to jump skyward and she couldn't look at Ty.

"Yes."

His reply was hoarse and clipped as she met his steady gaze.

A small, breathless whisper escaped as those passionate grey spheres blazed with a hunger that even someone with her lack of experience picked up on. Heat raced through her like a dust devil in July.

And just as quickly, his eyes became hooded, closed off and he inhaled sharply. "You look very nice, Miss Emma."

Her mouth was too parched to speak even if her befuddled mind came up with something to say.

"You sit there, Emma." Sarah pointed to the chair beside Ty, mischievous smile in place.

Without speaking, Ty held the chair for her.

A hard knock at the front door came as she sat down. Emma started to rise, but a light touch of Ty's hand on her shoulder stopped her. It was like being touched by lightning. She couldn't get up now if her life depended on it.

"I'm up, I'll get it."

She looked at her father and concern immediately overrode her reaction to Ty's hand on her shoulder. "Papa? Are you okay?"

"I'm good, Emma." He smiled at his daughter. "A mite tired is all." He looked past her toward the door. "Evenin', Hank."

She turned to find Hank Walker entering the dining room with Ty behind him, a pinched expression gracing the otherwise handsome face showed his displeasure at the arrival of this unexpected guest.

Hank walked in like he owned the place, much to Emma's irritation, and swaggered to her father.

"Rafe, my friend. Good to see you up and about." He shook hands with the older man then turned to Emma. "You didn't have to dress up on my account, but I am certainly glad you did."

He reached for her hand and she had to stop herself from jerking it away.

He pulled it to him, a little tighter than she thought necessary and brushed his lips across the top.

"You look good enough to eat," he whispered as he bent over her hand, eyes locking on the expanse of cleavage visible by the low cut gown. "Soon."

She jerked her hand away. "What are you doing here?"

"Emma." Rafe's soft rebuke was weak but determined. "I invited him to drop by anytime he wanted."

Hank smiled and started for the chair beside her.

Ty immediately sat down, leaving Hank no option but to sit at the other end of the table.

Lupe entered with a pot of coffee and flinched when she saw the newcomer.

"Lupe," said Rafe, "Please bring another plate for our guest."

Dinner was an ordeal for Emma. All her pains tonight were ruined by the appearance of Hank who watched her every move with calculated interest. His compliments, while nothing out of the ordinary, nonetheless made her uneasy and more than once, a look in his eye elicited an involuntary shiver.

Henry and Sarah carried most of the conversation while she and Ty spoke only when spoken to.

"Oh, I almost forgot why I came out this evening…other than to see Emma in such a beautiful dress, of course. You know, Em, you – "

"Only one person calls me Em," she snapped, "You're not him." Hearing it from his mouth made her want to toss the contents of her stomach.

His smile became pinched. "You really should remember you are a beautiful woman, Emma, not a man." He reached in his coat pocket and pulled out an envelope. "Telegram came for you this afternoon. I forgot to give it to you when I was here earlier." He stood and handed it to her. "Didn't know you were looking at new breeding stock."

"You read my message?" She sat up straighter, her temper sparking to life.

He had the audacity to chuckle. "This is a small town, Em…Emma. Word gets around fast. Especially when the biggest gossip in three counties is in charge of the telegraph." He returned to his seat and pulled a cigar from his pocket. "What kind of cattle are you trying to buy?"

"No smoking in the house."

Hank placed the cigar back in his pocket. "Something

else that will be changing soon."

"None of your business what I buy."

"It will be when we're married."

Sarah's gasp sounded like a gunshot in the small room. "Married?"

Rafe cleared his throat. "Hank here wants to marry Emma."

A deafening silence filled the room.

Emma stopped breathing. *Surely he won't force me to marry Walker?*

She heard Ty's quick inhale and from the corner of her eye, saw him stiffen.

"I've no wish to marry, Papa." Emma's voice shook and her hand clutched the unread telegram until it crumpled. *I don't want to marry him.*

"Your thirty days are up in a few days. You haven't found a husband."

Henry spoke for the first time, his glance darting from Ty to the old man. "Rafe, maybe you should discuss —"

"Nothin' to discuss. I gave her thirty days to find a husband and she chased off every man who showed up."

"Except me." Walker's conceited smile never reached his eyes. "I'm still here."

"And me." Ty's soft-spoken retort had everyone looking his way. "I'm still here."

CHAPTER
Ten

NO ONE WAS MORE SURPRISED BY HIS DECLARATION THAN Tyler Roundtree himself. *What the hell am I doing?* But one look at Walker and he knew — no way in hell would he let him anywhere near Emma. And if Rafe thought he would sit idly by and let it happen, he was sadly mistaken.

Emma's eyes locked on his, fear and uncertainty shimmering in their emerald depths.

He said the first thing that sprang to mind, deliberately using the pet name she forbade Walker to use. "I'm sorry I blurted it out, Em." He covered her clenched fist with his hand, squeezing lightly. "I know we are still discussing things."

No one spoke for several heartbeats, tension in the room palpable.

"That right, girl? You and Tyler here talking marriage?"

Rafe's question didn't immediately penetrate her

bewildered brain as she stared open-mouthed at the man who just told everyone they were getting maried.

Ty squeezed her hand and nodded toward her father. "Em?"

She blinked rapidly and drew in a breath. "Y-yes, we're… discussing it."

"Like hell." Walker's soft expletive pierced the silence like a knife.

Ty turned to his adversary, cold, grey eyes unblinking, and said nothing.

The stare-down continued until Rafe began coughing uncontrollably.

Emma moved to his side, hand rubbing his back until the spell abated. "Papa? Will a sip of water help?"

He shook his head slowly and gasped for air. "Ty…take me…back…to my room?"

Ty immediately got to his feet. "Of course."

Henry stood as well. "Need any help?"

"No, thanks. I got it."

Sarah covered her mouth with both hands. "Oh no!"

"Sweetheart? Are you going to be sick again?" Henry turned to his wife who simply nodded and staggered from the room, Henry beside her, leaving Emma and Walker alone.

By the time Ty reached the older man's room, his breathing had diminished to ragged gasps. He easily lifted him from the chair and settled him in bed. He turned, expecting to find Emma waiting and was surprised when he didn't.

He poured water into the basin and dipped a cloth in it, then gently wiped the older man's brow, holding the moist rag against his chapped lips.

"Shut…the   door…son."   Rafe's   weak   command

nonetheless brooked no opposition.

Ty did as instructed and returned to the chair by the bed.

"Emma is…everything…to me."

But you would give her to Walker without blinking an eye. He kept his face blank, revealing nothing of the barely controlled anger seething inside.

"Don't want…her to…marry…Walker."

His statement shocked him to the point he sat up straight and speared him with steely eyes. "Not the impression I got tonight."

He shook his head. "I'm dyin', Tyler, but I ain't blind." He wheezed in and out. "You make her smile." His jaw clinched, relaxed. "Want your word… won't mistreat her."

Ty looked at the old man and nodded. "You have my word, sir."

He sighed and closed his eyes.

Emma stared at the retreating figures, stunned to find herself alone with Walker who stood an arms-length away from her, his anger almost tangible.

"You think you can get rid of me so easily?" He ran his index finger down her cheek. "Think again."

She tried to step back, but quick as a rattler's strike, his hand gripped her neck tightly, mouth a tight line. "You belong to *me*." His lips curled into a cruel smile. "Your cowboy is good as dead."

Her heart raced like a thousand stampeding Longhorns, but she kept her voice steady. "I belong to no one."

His smile wasn't the least bit jovial. "You know what the

best part of taming a wild, spirited mustang is?" He didn't wait for a reply. "It's breaking her down till she knows who's boss." He licked his lips, stared at her bosom. "And I will break you, Emma. Make no mistake."

His grip loosened and she slapped his hand way, stepping back. "Get out."

He picked up his bowler off the corner cabinet and placed it on his head. "A lot of things are about to change around here." He pulled a cigar from his pocket. "Rafe isn't long for this world. You have to marry before he dies or your uncle gets this place." He stared at her, his eyes cold and calculating. "I aim to have you…and this ranch before that happens."

He struck a match to his cigar and sauntered out the door.

Her knees refused to hold her any longer and she sank to her chair. "Oh my, God."

CHAPTER
Eleven

MMA PLACED HER HEAD IN HER HANDS AND TRIED TO think, Walker's last words ringing in her ears. *I aim to have you… and this ranch before that happens.*

"Oh God…what am I going to do?"

"Em? Are you all right?"

Ty's apprehensive voice startled her and she jumped. "Y-yes." She sat up and smoothed down the front of her skirt. "I'm fine."

He took the chair beside her, knees all but touching her hip. "Where is everyone?"

She straightened. "Sarah took ill and Hank left."

"What did he say to upset you?"

She avoided looking at those all-seeing eyes. "Him breathing upsets me." Picking up the crumpled telegram, she read it, then passed it to Ty.

She hadn't mentioned the new Herefords she planned to

buy to anyone, not even her father and prepared to defend her decision to Ty. He was the foreman, had a right to know, but it was her ranch, her decision. *Will he understand?*

He scanned the short message then passed it back to her. "I met William Ikard in Ft. Worth a while back. Smart man. Dead set on bringing those Herefords to Texas. Said they were more adaptable to our climate and produced better beef, too." He passed the telegram back to her. "Be interesting to see how they handle East Texas weather."

It took a moment for her to realize he hadn't dismissed her bold move. "You're not upset?" It was more a statement than a question.

"It's your ranch, Em. Besides, you've obviously put a lot of thought into this or you wouldn't do it."

His support sent her spirits soring and she smiled for the first time all evening. "They really are beautiful animals, Ty. Ever seen one?"

He shook his head.

"They're from England and have this reddish body with a white face. Bulls can hit eighteen hundred pounds and cows twelve. The Ikard brothers brought some to Texas from Philadelphia. I bought a bull and two heifers from our cattle buyer in Ft. Worth."

He nodded and neither spoke for several heartbeats.

She chewed her lower lip, then looked at him. "Why did you do it?"

Ty hesitated. "Seemed like the thing to do at the time."

"Why?" She faced him, searched his face for the answer he didn't give.

"Walker's not right for you." He held up a hand when she stiffened. "I'm not trying to tell you how to run your life, but

I sense you don't like him. And he's trying to force himself on you." Ty shook his head. "I guess I thought if I said we were…a couple, he might back off."

"He won't." She immediately regretted her panicky response.

"What did he say, Em?"

She stood and paced around the dining room. "What am I going to do? Papa is worse every day."

"What exactly does the will state?"

"I haven't seen it, but my understanding is I must be married before…before Papa dies or my uncle gets Twin Oaks."

"Is it here? In the office maybe?"

"Why?" She was more curious than alarmed by his question.

"If we know exactly what the will says, then we will know what course of action you need to take."

"It's probably in the safe."

He followed her to the office and stood back while she opened the safe and pulled out the envelope marked *will* in her father's scratchy handwriting. She stared at it then handed it to Ty. "Please. I can't read it."

Ty pulled the sheaf of papers out and scanned them. "Well, it's actually a standard will in which everything goes to you. But there is an attachment, sort of like an addendum dated a few weeks ago that says you have to be married at the time of his death – and remain married for at least six months to secure title to the ranch."

"Why six months?"

"There's more." He paused and locked those mesmerizing eyes on hers. "If the marriage doesn't last six months, your husband will be entitled to one half of Twin Oaks. Should you die during that time, everything goes to him."

All the air whooshed out of her lungs and she clutched her chest. Her knees threatened to buckle, and she grabbed for the corner of the desk. "How could he do this to me?"

Ty grabbed her around the waist and led her to the small couch, then sat beside her. "Easy, Em, easy."

"He wants me to marry someone I detest, stay married to him for six months or give away half my ranch?"

"He doesn't want you to marry Walker."

"At dinner he said…he said…" she couldn't finish. The thought of marrying Hank Walker made her stomach roil.

"He doesn't want you to marry Walker." He paused, met her gaze. "He wants you to marry me."

CHAPTER
Twelve

EMMA STARED AT TY, COMPREHENSION SLOW IN COMING. "He told you that?"

He rested both elbows on his knees, hands clasped together as he looked toward the window. "Not exactly. He said Walker wasn't right for you and…asked me not to mistreat you." He looked at her then, his expression revealing nothing of his thoughts.

Butterflies, her constant companion of late, bounced around her stomach like hailstones, threatening to purge what little supper she had eaten. "And…?"

"I gave my word I wouldn't mistreat you."

Her heart skipped and fluttered, then settled into an uneasy rhythm. "Are y-you saying you…you would m-marry me?"

He faced her. "I believe when a man and woman get married it should be because they love each other and for always."

He paused. "I'm a hard man, Em, set in my ways. I'm thirty-seven…fought a horrific war, done things I ain't proud of." He lowered his head, then raised it again. "I'm tired of roaming, without roots. I didn't realize it until recently but, well, I want a home. A family." He took a breath, blew it out slowly. "I want you."

Intense, smoldering eyes held her captive. She struggled for air, heart pounding so hard she expected it to break through her chest at any moment.

"As a man wants a woman."

Excitement flowed through her like hot lava, stealing her voice. *He wants me…as a man wants a woman.*

"Marriages like this are not uncommon." His words were hoarse and strained.

"Mable Baker at the general store was a mail order bride." She failed to keep the squeakiness from her voice.

He nodded, locking and unlocking his fingers. "I'll be a good and faithful husband. I'll work hard to make this place whatever you want it to be." He waited a beat, then continued, "But, if we do this, I don't want there to be any misconceptions about what will happen. I want a *real* marriage." He reached for her hand, caressed it lightly. "Do you understand what I mean?"

Warmth flooded her face, as she swallowed hard and nodded.

"I suspect you aren't…experienced." He rubbed his thumb lightly over her knuckles. "And I will never, ever force myself on you. But at some point, I hope sooner rather than later, I *will* expect us to be man and wife. In every way."

Her lips parted on a soft gasp but she couldn't look away.

"Understand this, too." His eyes bored into hers. "Twin

Oaks is a prime piece of land. No question about it; but that's not what I want. If something happens and we part, whether it's in six months or six years, I want nothing that belongs to you." He paused. "Unless we have a child. Whether we are together or not, I will never leave my child without a father. Never."

She expected her cheeks to burst into flames any second now. He didn't mince words.

"I reckon you need some time to think so I'll say goodnight." Ty headed for the door.

"No."

He turned, jaw tight, his face grim. "No? You'd rather marry Walker?"

"What? No!" She jumped up from the couch, hands fisting in her skirt. "I'd drink a gallon of pond scum first."

"Then…?"

"I…I don't need to think about it."

"You don't?"

"N-no." She crossed her arms over her chest, briefly met his gaze. "I-I'll do it." She looked him in the eye. "I'll marry you."

"I meant what I said, Emma Rose. I want a real marriage."

"I-I know." She bit her lower lip. "But there's some things – important things—you need to know…before *you* decide. Because, well, because you might change your mind."

She saw him stiffen, clench his jaw. "I'm listening."

Oh God. How do I tell him? "You're right…about…the experience part." She avoided looking at him, cheeks so hot she expected blood to start oozing out. "Hell, I ain't never even been kissed. Well, Papa but his don't count." She rolled the skirt in her hands until a good foot of the petticoat showed, then blurted out the dreaded words. "And… I-I can't cook."

Ty blinked twice, staring at the top of her lowered head. *She's never been kissed and she can't cook.* That's her important things? "You can't cook?"

She shook her head. "I can do little stuff like fry bacon and eggs, but not much more. Oh, and coffee. I can make coffee."

He worked hard not to grin. *If she ain't the cutest thing I've ever seen.* "And you think those things would affect my decision?"

She glanced up briefly, and looked away. "You said you want a real wife. A real wife should know how to cook and to..to…you know."

"Look at me, Em."

When she didn't respond, he put his finger under her chin and tilted her face up.

She chewed her lower lip, eyes shimmering, then straightened her spine and met his gaze full on. "I'll be twenty-six in a couple of months. I spent my whole life learnin' how to run this ranch. But I don't know anything about… bein' a woman." She averted her face, bright spots of color on each cheek. "You need to know that upfront. And, I'm, well, not proper, I guess cause I cuss."

This is the damnedest conversation I've ever had in my life. His finger made a raspy sound as he scratched the beard stubble on his jaw. "Well, I can cook some and unless Lupe leaves, we won't starve."

She looked at him and his heart rate went through the

roof. *A man could get lost in those mossy-green depths.*

Her gaze dropped his mouth, and she licked her lips, causing his groin to become painfully tight. He had to clear his throat— twice, before he could speak. "As for the other, well…there's some things I can teach you, when you're ready. That is, if you want me to."

"You can?" she whispered.

Her voice, soft and sexy on a good day, dropped an octave and potent desire careened through him. Not trusting himself to speak, he nodded.

"What about…um, kissing?"

He reminded himself to breathe. "It ain't hard."

She stepped toward him. "I want to know what…what it feels like…first." Her voice shuddered. "If it's not too much trouble."

Oh shit.

Those tantalizing dots of green shimmered with uncertainty as they held his gaze.

"Would you kiss me, Ty? Please?"

Holy shit.

CHAPTER
Thirteen

Ty's heart slammed so hard and fast he feared it would burst from the strain. He tried to talk but speaking and breathing at the same time wasn't possible. He closed the distance between them, trembling hands cupped her face.

Her voice dropped to a hushed whisper. "What do I do?"

He groaned. "Nothing. Just let me show you what it feels like."

She nodded, gaze riveted on his mouth as he leaned down.

She glanced up and the shock of discovery hit him full force. *My God…she has no idea how beautiful she is.*

"I saw Sarah put her arms around Henry's neck once." She spoke tentatively as tough testing the idea. "Should I do that?"

Groin tight as a bowstring, he forced out a reply. "Only if you want to."

A pensive shimmer in the shadow of her eyes, she gently slid her hands up his chest, and around his neck, igniting a flash fire of need he fought to contain.

He lowered his head, intending a light brush of her lips, a chaste kiss to get her accustomed to the feel of him.

That was the plan, which immediately disintegrated the minute their lips met.

Soft and moist, she tasted like the sweetest berries. His raging desire soared when she shuddered against him. Stopping wasn't an option. He may as well try and touch the moon.

A small, breathless whisper escaped as he claimed her lips again, using his tongue to urge them wider.

She clutched at him, obligingly opened her mouth to allow him entry.

He took what she offered, his tongue dipping inside to explore the velvety softness, skimming the tip of hers and it twitched in response…then shyly touched his.

Reason vanished.

He craved more.

His hands dropped to her waist then slid down to her hips, pulling her tight against his hardness.

She tensed, then pressed herself to him, fingers digging into his shoulders.

He plundered her mouth, eliciting a soft moan that nearly undid him, but, thankfully, also brought his senses back. *Slow down. Wrong time. Wrong place.*

He pulled back, gulped air like a downing man breaking the water's surface, then leaned his forehead against hers as he waited for his heart rate to return to normal.

"Damn."

The soft expletive from Emma made him pull back and look at her. "I'm sorry…I shouldn't…did I hurt you?"

Those stunning orbs met his full on and had the same effect as being butted in the gut by a bull.

He was done for.

"No. I…Thank you."

Unexpected, her comment took a moment to register and when it did, he grinned. "You're welcome."

She ducked her head, skimmed her hands down his shoulders, and over his arms before dropping them to her sides.

Everywhere she touched, he burned.

"I best go check on Papa." She stopped, eyes directed behind him.

He turned and saw Henry standing in the doorway, mouth set in a tight, angry line.

"Emma, Sarah is asking for you."

His terse voice radiated tension and Ty braced himself for what would come next.

"Of course. I need to check on Papa first." She looked at Ty and smiled. "Night, Ty. Good night, Henry."

"Night, Emma."

Henry waited until the door shut behind her. "What the hell are you doing?"

Ty gritted his teeth, tried to gain some control of his emotions before replying. "Well, since you ain't blind or stupid, I reckon you know."

"She's like a sister to me and Sarah. I don't wanna see her get hurt."

"Neither do I."

"How many times have you told me you're not the

settling down kind?"

"Things change. People change."

Henry stood with hands fisted at his sides, and didn't speak for several moments. Then, he bowed his head and blew out a long, slow breath. "She smiled, Ty." He looked at his friend. "Just now. I've never seen her smile like that."

"That's what Rafe said so I'm guessin' it's a good thing."

Henry straightened, brown eyes drilling into him. "What are your intentions?"

Ty snorted. "My intentions? What are you...her father now?"

"She's family, dammit. What are your intentions?"

Ty ran calloused fingers through his hair. "I want it all."

Henry stiffened, his voice hard as steel. "You'd take a sweet girl like Emma just to get her ranch?"

Ty whirled on his friend. "What the hell kinda man do you think I am?"

When he didn't reply, Ty raised his hands in the air. "Shit, Henry. I thought you knew me better than that." He inhaled, blew it out slowly. "I'm tired of floating around. I want what you have...a home, a family." He met Henry's fierce gaze. "I want Emma." He held up his hand to silence any retort. "And I already told her if things didn't work out, I wanted no part of anything belonging to her."

"Do you love her?"

I want her so bad my teeth hurt.

"Hell, I don't know as I even know what love is, but I'm right fond of her." He thought of kissing her, the passion he sensed waiting to be discovered and tamped down the rush of desire it triggered. "She's a pistol for sure with enough grit to go bear huntin' with a switch." He rolled his head from side to side. "Can't say I love her any more 'n she loves me, but she's agreeable to the deal."

Henry stared at him for several heartbeats, then nodded, apparently satisfied with his answer. "What about Walker? That sonofabitch is trouble if ever I saw it."

"He is for a fact and for damn sure she won't be alone with him again."

"Why? Did something happen?"

"I think so but she wouldn't tell me what." Ty walked to the cabinet in the corner. "I need a drink. You?"

"Yeah, thanks."

He poured two glasses of Rafe's whiskey and passed one to his companion.

Henry lifted his in a toast, his roguish smile making the dimple in his right cheek deeper. "To happily ever after."

"Humphf."

★ ★ ★

Emma walked slowly, praying her racing heart would soon return to normal. Her hands still tingled from resting on his shoulders, and her lips…oh God, she tasted him still. *If all men kiss like him, I've been missing out.*

She peeked in on her father, glad to find he slept peacefully. She did not want to explain anything to him, not when her emotions were in such an uproar. Sarah was going to be bad enough.

She took a deep breath, tapped on the door of Sarah's room, and waited for the quiet "Come in." Her friend sat in a rocker by the window, a shawl over her shoulders.

"Hey. Feeling better?"

Sarah pushed herself out the chair and hurried to Emma. "What happened after I left? Are you and Ty really getting married? What did that awful man have to say about it?"

Emma smiled. "One question at a time and you need to sit back down."

She guided Sarah to the rocker then pulled a chair away from the fireplace to sit beside her.

"Start at the beginning," ordered Sarah, "and don't leave anything out."

Ten minutes later, her friend stared open-mouthed as Emma ended her story. "And, well, we kinda kissed." *Kinda? I'm pretty sure I was thoroughly kissed.*

Sarah stared without speaking for so long Emma became concerned. "What's wrong? You haven't said a word."

Her friend jiggled her head, opened her mouth, closed it, and then placed a hand over her lips.

"Oh no!" Emma looked around for the chamber pot. "Are you going to be sick again?"

"You *let* him kiss you?" Sarah's awestruck whisper was accompanied by enlarged eyes. "You, Emma Rose Marshall; the woman who has never allowed a man within arms-length of her, let one *kiss* you?"

"Well, if you must know, I sorta asked him to."

Sarah sputtered, leaned forward. "What did you say?"

Emma fiddled with her skirt, avoided looking at her. "I wanted to know…I…asked him to and, well, he did." *My lips still tingle.*

"And?" Sarah scooted to the edge of her chair, reached for Emma's hands. "What did you think?"

A timid smile curled up the edges of her mouth. "It was nice."

"Just nice?" Sarah snorted. "Then he didn't do it right." She sat back in the chair, hands rubbing her swollen belly. "I swear, Henry can make my toes curl when he kisses me the way man kisses a woman when he…" she paused, her smile seductive, "has something on his mind."

The dreaded warmth returned to Emma's cheeks with a vengeance, and she looked away. "He did it right. I think. I mean…"

She grabbed Emma's hands again. "I want details. How did he do it? What did you do? How did you feel?"

Emma frowned. "I can't tell you all that."

"We've told each other practically everything all our lives. And I can see I will have to be more specific now since you are getting married but that can wait. Right now, I want to know about the kiss."

The next few minutes were devoted to analyzing Ty's ability to kiss, much to the delight of Sarah and the total embarrassment of Emma.

"But you liked it, didn't you? Kissing him?"

"Uh-huh."

"And you know where kissing leads, right?"

"Well, yes, I guess." She shrugged, unwilling to admit even to her best friend, her lack of experience in that area. "I know what horses and cows do. I guess it's the same more or less with people."

Sarah lowered her head to her hands. "Oh Lord, you don't know nothin' do you?"

CHAPTER
Fourteen

EMMA SAT IN THE OLD ROCKER ON THE PORCH LISTENING to the sounds of the night, a single thought rolling through her mind: *I'm getting married tomorrow.*

The moon hung low in the sky, just over the top of the barn illuminating the area with a misty glow. The last two days were a challenge. First, dealing with Rafe, who seemed surprisingly supportive of her marrying Ty and second, dealing with Leo and the other hands. Leo wasted no time in saying he would be moving on after the round up. She hated to see him go and considered asking him to stay but decided it would be best if he didn't.

Ty didn't say much beyond work related things which bothered her a lot. *Was he second-guessing his decision? Would he change his mind?*

Sarah, on the other hand, had plenty to say and Emma's cheeks still burned from their last conversation. Sarah's adamant declaration of the *next time will be wonderful* had Emma covering her ears. How on earth could she be like that with Ty?

She shuddered. There was so much more to this marriage stuff than she thought. She stood, stopping when she saw her husband-to-be watching from the end of the porch.

"Ty. I didn't hear you walk up."

He walked toward her. "Sure is peaceful tonight."

Her stomach clinched as images of what Sarah had regaled her with earlier formed in her mind. "Um, yes it is."

He stopped a few feet away, locked those mesmerizing eyes on her, gluing Emma's feet to the floor.

"What did Walker say the other night?"

Not at all what she expected him to say and it caught her off guard. "What? Oh, nothing important."

He took a step closer, his velvety voice raising gooseflesh on her arms.

"I will never, *ever* lie to you, Em." He paused. "And I expect the same in return. What did he say?"

She bit her lower lip, heaved a sigh. "He said I wouldn't be rid of him so easily." She squared her shoulders. "And that you were good as dead."

He nodded. "Figured as much." He closed the short distance between them, ran a finger down her cheek.

She couldn't stop the sudden gasp or the shiver than ran through her.

"I don't trust him, especially where you're concerned." He ran his thumb over her trembling lips. "Stay away from him."

It took a moment for his words to penetrate the veil of inexperienced desire clouding her mind, and she took a step back. "Stay away from him? Are you telling me what to do?"

"I'm telling you he's bad news, which you are smart enough to know."

"But not smart enough to know to stay away from him unless you tell me to?" She stood ramrod straight, hands fisted at her sides, voice rife with controlled anger.

She saw his jaw clench and storm clouds gather in those fearsome grey spheres, but didn't back down. They weren't even married yet and already he tried to control her. She wouldn't have it. Not for a minute.

"Not sure why you think being concerned for your safety is telling you what to do, but you best get used to it."

Before she uttered the scathing rebuttal he deserved…as soon as she found her voice, he walked away.

Ty gritted his teeth so hard his jaw hurt. *Damn stubborn-ass woman.*

Not at all how he envisioned the evening ending. The thought of kissing her again dug under his skin like a hidden tick. Just the thought of it made his body throb with need.

But her damn pigheaded pride interfered and it ended before it even started. *Prickly as a cactus is right…but damned if I don't like her fiery spirit, too.*

Trouble was, he liked everything about her. The way her infrequent smiles lit up her face and made his stomach flip over. The way her eyes flashed when riled made him wonder what would happen if all that fire were directed to more enjoyable tasks.

He rested his forearms across the top rail of the corral and exhaled slowly, willing his aching body to relax. They would be married tomorrow; if the wedding night didn't happen soon after, he wasn't sure he would make it. But he gave his word he wouldn't push and would wait if it killed him. Considering his state at the moment, it probably would.

He sensed when she came up behind him though she didn't speak at first.

"…what did you mean about *get used to it*?"

Something in her voice alerted him. Uncertainty? Fear? Cautious, he turned, one arm still resting on the rail, and was struck mute. Moonlight softened her features and made starlight twinkle in her eyes. Her hair fell in glorious waves over her shoulders and that damn top button called him like a siren. *Why is it I find her most appealing in those damn jeans?*

He tried to speak but nothing came out. He cleared his throat, looked at the barn in the distance and not the moonlit angel in front of him. Finally, his voice returned. "What are you afraid of?"

She jerked and drew his attention back to her face where shock and surprise made her eyes widen, and her lips quiver. "I don't know what you're talking about."

She spun around and he grabbed her arm, moved in front and placed his hands on her shoulders. "No lies, Emma."

Lips a tight line, she said nothing.

He paused, clenched his jaw, then relaxed it. "You are a beautiful, strong and self-reliant woman."

Her brows lifted and her mouth dropped open.

"You have such a…a fire in you…I don't ever want to see that fire banked or put out." *I want to know the pleasure side of that fire.* "Just because I say do something or don't do something, doesn't mean I'm trying to order you around. I'll be your husband." He dropped his hands and took a step back, the urge to kiss her again so strong it made him quake.

"A man looks out for his wife, protects her, even when it means protecting her from herself. I don't know any other way." He shoved his hands in his pockets. "So, you'll just have to accept me as I am and I'll do the same for you. Our differences will no doubt result in some…disagreements." Visions of making up after those disagreements brought a slow smile to his face. "But I think the making up afterwards will be worth it."

Moonlight danced in the emerald pools fixed on him. "Making up?" she whispered.

He nodded, took a step forward. "When we disagree, and I don't doubt for one minute there will be some dandies, the anger won't last, not when you look at me like that."

"H-how am I-I looking?"

He stood close enough to see the passion-darkened pupils, smell the faint aroma of roses in her hair. "Like you want me to kiss you."

"I-I do."

So he did.

CHAPTER
Fifteen

EMMA STARED AT THE STRANGER REFLECTED IN THE mirror. *That can't be me.*

Thanks to Lupe, her mother's peach silk gown fit beautifully. Handmade ivory lace from her grandmother's wedding dress formed a delicate topping over the bodice, highlighted by a single peach rose nestled between her breasts. A full skirt cascaded from the empire waist under an open tiered silk overlay decorated with delicate embroidery and more lace, then melted into a short train in the back. An off-the-shoulder neckline and short sleeves emphasized a graceful neck and ample bosom.

Lupe's talented hands swept her hair into beautiful rolls and curls adorned with pale pink rose accents.

Sarah's pixie face displayed an ear-to-ear smile. "You are so beautiful."

"*Si,* Miss Emma," agreed Lupe. "Señor Ty will be very

happy to see this."

Emma continued to stare at her reflection. "Lupe?" She turned to the woman who'd tended the family all her life. "Do I really look like her? My mother? I don't remember anymore."

"*Si*, you look much like her, Miss Emma."

Thunder rumbled in the distance drawing her attention to the window. Outside, townspeople milled around the yard in preparation for the celebration. Short notice or not, a party was a party and they turned out for it.

"Oh no, please," she whispered to no one in particular, "no rain today."

"Do not worry, Miss Emma," said Lupe as she went about straightening the room. "The rain will not come until tonight."

Emma didn't turn around as she spoke to Sarah. "How much longer?"

"Any minute now. Henry will come when they are ready."

Henry would escort her down to the living room where her father and Ty waited.

She gasped and turned to Sarah. "What if I'm making a mistake?"

"Jitters are normal, Emma." She patted her hand. "Ty's a good man, not as handsome as my Henry of course, but nice to look at, and he will be good to you."

He doesn't love me.

"I know you are nervous about all this but I also know you have feelings for Ty," she held up her hand to silence a reply, "whether you are ready to admit it or not. Personally, I think the two of you are perfect for one another."

A light knock on the door preceded Henry's soft,

"Everything's ready."

"Here we go!" Sarah kissed her friend on the cheek. "Everything will be fine. You'll see." She opened the door and smiled at her husband. "I'll see you downstairs."

Henry entered and kissed her on the cheek. "You look wonderful, Emma."

She smoothed down the front of the dress. "It was my mother's wedding dress."

"It's beautiful. And so are you. Ty is a lucky man."

Suddenly, she swayed and gasped for air. Her heart pounded so hard she sensed each beat in her ears.

Henry grabbed her around the waist. "Easy, Emma, easy." He moved her toward the nearest chair. "Just relax, try to take a deep breath and let it out slowly."

She nodded, then inhaled a ragged breath, blowing it out through pursed lips.

"Good girl. Now do it again."

One breath, then another. Each one easier than the one before. "I'm sorry. I don't know what came over me."

He smiled. "If I remember right, the same thing that came over Sarah on our wedding day. Except you didn't actually faint."

She sniffed. "I'd forgotten she fainted."

He knelt down in front of her. "Ty is a fine man, Emma; my best friend in the whole world. But if you aren't absolutely certain about this, you don't have to do it."

She thought about Ty…his strength, his support…his kisses…and his promise of more to being husband and wife he could teach her, and knew she would do it. Not to satisfy her father's ridiculous ultimatum or the morbid curiosity of the townspeople in attendance but because she *really* wanted to.

She loved him.

The realization made her heart stutter and skip, and perspiration coated her palms. *I've loved him from the beginning.*

She shook her head. "No. I want to do this." She stood and squared her shoulders. "I'm ready."

She picked up the bouquet of wildflowers Sarah made, linked her arm with Henry's, and prepared to meet her fate.

Ty tugged at the too-tight shirt collar and surveyed the crowded room. He'd overheard enough to know quite a few attended just to see who would actually marry *that wild Marshall girl*. Others, like the Barkers from the mercantile, expressed genuine happiness for her.

When Sarah and Lupe rushed in, his mouth went dry. *I'm getting married.*

Reverend Johnson guided him to the flower-draped mantel where Rafe waited.

Someone, he thought maybe the preacher's wife, played a familiar, melodic song on the piano in the corner. Beethoven's *Fur Elise*. One of his mother's favorites, she played it often. As the musical notes filled the air, fond memories of days long past soothed his soul. *A good omen.*

A rustle of movement filled the crowed parlor along with a collective gasp as Henry walked through the doorway with Emma. She paused and the room went silent. Her gaze found Ty and she smiled serenely, lifted her head high, and glided toward him.

An unexpected tempo set up in Ty's chest, and took his breath away as he gazed at the vision before him.

She moved with an instinctive elegance and grace befitting any Georgia belle. *Mother would've adored you.* Stopping when they reached her father, she bent down and kissed his forehead as tears rolled down his cheeks. She placed a hand on his shoulder and faced forward.

"Who gives this woman to be married?" The preacher's droll voice barely penetrated Ty's over-stimulated brain.

"I do," said Rafe. He took her hand, brushed his lips across the back and murmured, "You are so beautiful, Emma-girl. So beautiful." Then, he pushed her hand toward Ty.

When he took it in his, he noted the tremble, the coolness, the sketchy breathing and vowed to himself he would do his absolute best to make her happy.

Henry moved Rafe's chair and the brief ceremony was over in a matter of minutes.

"You may now kiss the bride."

The reverend's directive, delivered in the same tiresome tone, hit home. *I'm a married man now.*

From the corner of his eye, he saw the straining necks of those gathered, waiting for this moment, and decided they would get no exhibition from him. The kiss was brief, but a whispered promise heightened the color on her cheeks. "A better one comes later."

Rafe shook Ty's hand, followed by Henry.

Sarah grabbed her in a fierce hug. "Congratulations to you both."

The sea of well-wishers and gossip mongers swallowed them up in an instant.

Ty gave up trying to remember names as Emma, smile attentive, introduced him to one person after another.

They made their way through the crowd which soon

filtered outside where temporary tables laden with every manner of food available were set up under the two massive live oaks for which the ranch was named.

Ty seized the opportunity and pulled her into the kitchen.

She slipped her hand from his and went to the crock on the counter.

He watched, spellbound as she immersed the dipper, brought it to her mouth and took a long, slow drink. A dribble found its way out and rolled over a plump, lower lip. She pulled the dipper back, and her tongue licked at the trail, sending rivulets of heat coursing through him. She took another long drink before swiping the remaining droplets away, her gentle laugh music to his ears and fodder for his growing desire.

"Didn't realize how thirsty I was. Want some?" She held out the dipper to him.

He returned it to the crock. "I promised you a better kiss."

He cupped her face and claimed her lips with a deep, sensual kiss as his tongue invaded her mouth, withdrew and invaded again. He deepened the kiss, and she clutched his arms, moved against him, tentative at first, then more firmly, visions of a real wedding night immediately forming. He snuffed them out. Despite her acceptance and expanding participation in his kisses, she wasn't ready.

Unfortunately for him, he passed *ready* a long time ago.

His body pulsed with need. Every inch of him wanted her, craved her, and wouldn't be satisfied until he had her. Maybe not even then. He needed to get himself under control before they re-joined their guests.

Control? Hell, who was he kidding? *Damn thing could*

hammer nails right now.

He ended the kiss, his breath a ragged gasp as he struggled to restrain himself. "I, uh, need a few minutes before I join the party."

The reason for his request pressed against her and she stepped back, those green orbs darkened with passion, her chest rising and falling in an irregular rhythm. Her lips, swollen from his kisses, drew his gaze, as her tongue, pink and slick, rolled over them like a cat lapping cream.

He shut his eyes, unable to stop the groan lodged in his throat.

Neither spoke until the uneven puffing dissipated and some semblance of regular breathing returned.

She broke the tense silence. "I know I'm…not what you expected in a wife…not a proper lady…but, thank you. For doing this." She stopped, bit her lip and looked away.

He tilted her chin up to meet his gaze, voice husky with barely controlled need, his body still suffering the effects of that potent kiss. "I don't know what you've been told before, but there is nothing wrong with you. Nothing."

"I cuss. Ladies don't cuss. And I dress like man."

He stood back, drank in every line, every curve, made no effort to hide the fact he pictured what lay beneath the silky garment. "You respond like a woman when I kiss you, your body feels like a woman when I touch it." He smiled. "And for damn sure you look like one tonight. I guarantee you there ain't man around here who has seen you in those jeans that don't know you're a woman." His grin broadened, "In fact, I might have to put a stop to it just so I won't need to kick someone's ass for ogling yours."

The minute he saw her lips tighten and her eyes narrow,

he knew he'd said something wrong though he had no idea what. *Well shit. Not married an hour and already pissed her off.*

"And how do you plan to do that? Beat me? Break me down?" She whirled and started for the door.

He grabbed her arm. "Wait."

Her voice rose, vibrated with tension. "I won't be broken." She jerked free and stared at him, eyes blazing.

"Broken? What the hell are you talking about?"

She stumbled back, hand clasped over her mouth.

"What do you mean you won't be broken?"

"N-nothing…I just meant I won't be ordered around."

The tightness of her features, the way her voice shook said there was more to this than being order around. Why wouldn't she tell him the rest?

He rubbed his face and hissed out a long breath. "I admit we don't know each other very well, but by now you should at least know I would never hurt you. And for damn sure, I've no desire to break you."

He spun around and stomped out the back door.

CHAPTER
Sixteen

EMMA WATCHED HER NEW HUSBAND LEAVE, FLINCHING when the door slammed behind him. Honesty forced her to admit what Walker said the other night got to her. So much so, she had nightmares about it.

She knew Ty wasn't like him at all, but things were so far over her head right now she couldn't think straight. Warring emotions twisted like knots in a rope leaving her off-balance. The heady rush of desire she experienced at the mere sight of Ty excited and frightened her. His kisses had the power to rob her of all rational thought. The control she prided herself on inched away and that alarmed her. She would never be controlled by someone else. Ever.

Walker said he would break me...

With a dejected sigh, she stepped out onto the porch, and froze.

Hank Walker stood on the top step.

"Hello, Emma." He moved toward her. "Been looking for you." He took another step. "Wanted to make sure I got to kiss the bride like everyone else."

She shuffled back. "Stay away from me." She receded another step, stopped by the wall behind her. She saw the evil intent in his eyes he made no effort to hide.

He ran a finger down her cheek. "I admit I'm disappointed he gets you first, but then first timers are so tedious." He brushed his thumb over her lower lip, pressing hard enough her teeth bit into the tender flesh. "I'll let him take the edge off," he whispered, "then show you how a real man handles a woman who doesn't know her place."

She pushed against his chest, so scared she couldn't utter a sound. *Please! Someone help me!*

"Take your hands off my wife."

Emma never heard that cold, hard tone in his voice before and nearly dropped to the floor with relief.

Walker shifted toward the steps, and smiled. "Why I merely offered my congratulations to the new bride." He hooked his thumbs into his belt, looking down at Ty. "No harm in that."

He glanced back at Emma and winked out of Ty's view, then stepped off the porch and headed for the front yard, whistling.

Ty appeared at her side in a heartbeat, hands on her shoulders. "Are you all right? Did he hurt you?"

She clung to his shirt front, knees shaking so badly she feared falling to the floor.

"What did he do, Em? Answer me."

"N-nothing….he just wanted t-to s-say congratulations."

"Bull shit."

She licked her lips, tasted the blood on them, then saw him jerk up, focused on her mouth.

"That sonofabitch! I'll kill him."

He turned, and she grabbed his hand. "No, Ty, please. It…it's not what you think. I was frightened and I - I bit my lip. That's all. I bit my lip."

His gaze was lethal, disbelief etched into the tight lines around his mouth.

"Ty, please. Don't let him ruin this day for me. For us."

Jaw clenched, mouth tight, his gaze bored into hers. "This ain't over, Em. I *will* know what he said."

He grunted and pulled her to him, his arms strong and warm as he cradled her head on his shoulder. "I'm sorry for whatever I said before to upset you. I…well, I was just teasing."

Her heart melted. He really didn't want to control her, not like Walker did.

She pulled back and looked at him. "I'm sorry I react-ed the way I did. I'm a bundle of nerves today." Her tongue traced her lower lip, a piece of smile curled the edges up. "So, does this mean we can make up now?"

His smile, slow in coming, stole her breath. "Yeah. We can make up now."

His kiss was a gentle, yet heated brushing of the lips that foretold of things to come.

She slid her arms around his neck, returning his prac-ticed ardor with her own fledgling enthusiasm. A soft groan emanated from his throat and she pressed herself more fully against him. His hands gripped her hips and anchored her to him, where the heat of his arousal filtered through her gown.

She experienced a moment of panic. *Oh my God! He will*

expect me to…to…

He must have sensed her inner withdrawal because he ended the kiss, slid his hands up her back to rest on her waist, easing their bodies apart. He hissed in a breath. "I meant what I said, Em."

When she did not immediately look at him, he raised her chin with his finger. "Not until you are ready."

She gulped, bobbed her head.

His sensual smile sent heat pooling in her middle, unseasoned desire sending ripples of sensation through her.

"But I aim to do what I can to hurry that day along."

"Y-you d-do?"

He nodded. "I want you to get used to me touching you."

He brushed his fingers down her neck, her chest and across her breast. He palmed its fullness through the light material, rubbing his thumb over the hardened peak and she gasped, then leaned into his intimate caress.

"So I aim to touch you, and kiss you every chance I get. I don't care who's around to see it. Even the hands."

She winced. She didn't want them to think less of her because of Ty.

"You're my wife now. The men will understand and expect us to act a certain way." He paused. "Even Leo."

She looked down, then back up at him. "I never encouraged him. I promise."

"I know."

He fixed those intense slate eyes on her, the scar on his cheek adding a strange element of danger to him. Her pulse quickened and heat settled in her middle.

"And, if you are of a mind to, you can do the same."

She blinked. Twice. Kiss him? Touch him? In front

of others? "You want me to k-kiss y-you? In front of other people?"

His eyes crinkled around the edges when he smiled, sending those damn butterflies on another furious rampage.

"Only if you're of a mind to."

"I…rather like kissing you," she murmured softly, eyes averted. "I'm just not certain I can do it front of anyone." She gnawed her sore lip, "But it would probably be okay if you, well, if you kissed me."

"Your guests are starting to wonder if the honeymoon started already."

Henry's jovial proclamation had her cheeks burning.

"I was sent to find you so some serious partying can happen before those clouds dump on us." A rumble of thunder in the distance punctuated his remark. "Old timers are saying it's gonna be a frog floater by dark."

Ty crooked his elbow, and she placed her arm through it. "Well, wife, shall we go see to our guests?"

She gave him a nervous smile. "Absolutely…husband."

CHAPTER
Seventeen

B Y THE TIME THE FIRST FAT RAINDROPS FELL, THE LAST OF the wedding guests were on their way home. Emma may not cook, she did clean and, as was the custom, all the ladies pitched in to help and in no time at all, everything was in order.

She could no longer delay the inevitable.

"Guess we're done," she said to Lupe. "Ty and the crew are putting the tables away."

"Such a nice wedding, Miss Emma. Your mother would be so happy for you."

"I hope so." *Even though it's not a love-match...on his part.*

Lupe grabbed her shawl from the hook by the door. "I best get home before the bottom falls out." She smiled as she started out the door. "Do not worry so. Everything will be fine. You will see."

Worried did not begin to describe how she felt about the coming night.

She was married.

Her new husband would be coming inside at any moment and…what? Visions of things Sarah hinted about danced in her head. Just thinking about them sent her heart rate soaring and her stomach to flutter and dance. *Can I really do that with Ty?*

On the one hand, anxiety consumed her but on the other, curiosity tormented her. Was it as wonderful as Sarah led her to believe or something she simply endured as Mable said? Each day, she experienced some new sensation around him. He made her feel things she had never experienced before, made her want to know what the next step would be.

But one thing Sarah said haunted her. There would be pain the first time, maybe quite intense but over quickly, and followed by pleasure. However, Emma had trouble believing pain and pleasure co-existed. Further questioning produced no satisfactory answers.

Her mind churned with uncertainties for which she had no solutions.

Feet like leaden weights, she turned and trudged up the stairs.

Ty stood on the front porch, listening to the rumble of thunder as it drew ever closer, the spattering of rain coming in fits and starts, and knew to his soul, he was home. He had known it for some time just wouldn't let himself believe it. Something about this place drew him in. Emma, certainly, but it went beyond that, though he couldn't actually put it into words.

He never thought it would happen, but he had a home.

At last.

He swirled the whiskey in his glass then took a healthy drink, savoring the sharp-tasting liquid as it slid down his throat. His nerves were stressed to the max and he delayed going upstairs as long as he dared. He had no idea what would happen when Emma discovered he intended to spend the night in her bed whether they consummated the marriage or not.

He certainly had high hopes, but he was also a realist. While he might be ready, she wasn't.

Did he love his new wife? He cared for her, respected her and Lord knows he wanted – needed – her as much as his next breath. And while she may not realize it yet, she had similar feelings for him; he sensed it in her touch, the way she reacted to his kisses, the way she looked at him when she thought he didn't notice.

Could he keep his promise? Remain aloof until she wanted to move forward? "God I hope so," he whispered to the night wind, "I hope so."

A few minutes later, he stood in front of her – their - bedroom door, uncertainty tying his stomach in knots. *The hell with it.* Two quick raps on the door and he walked in.

She sat on the edge of the bed, that glorious mass of curls unbound and flowing down her back, shoulders slumped, hands clasped in front as if in prayer.

My God. She looks like she's going to the gallows.

"Emma?" He walked toward her. "What's wrong?" *Like I don't know.*

"I can't do it."

Shit.

"I thought I made myself clear. You don't have to do anything you don't want to."

She straightened but did not face him. "I can't get undressed."

His experience with proper women was basically non-existent so he assumed she referred to getting undressed with him in the room.

"I see. I'll go downstairs a bit and give you some privacy."

"No!"

The exasperation unmistakable in that one word stopped him in his tracks. He had no idea what to say so wisely said nothing.

She shifted on the edge of the bed, and her hands fisted in the covers. "The damn buttons are in the back." She glanced toward him and looked away. "I can't reach them."

"…Oh."

The slow, steady hiss as she expelled a long breath spoke volumes.

"Well…ummm…"

She pushed herself up, and turned her back to him, raking her hair over one shoulder. "Please be careful with the buttons," she whispered. "This was my mother's dress."

He wavered, heart pounding furiously, then closed the distance between them. His hands trembled as he reached for the top button; fingers tingling from contact with creamy flesh and desire burst through him like a cannon, causing his whole body to ache with need.

She inhaled sharply, and he felt a shiver run through her. *Please give me strength.*

The buttons seemed like tiny pebbles in his large hands

and he had a measure of difficulty maneuvering them through the delicate opening, but one by one, he made his way down the back, revealing a light corset and chemise underneath.

Three buttons remained. He forced his hands to move, slid each tiny disc through the opening and moved to the next, trying his best not to think about sliding anything anywhere.

She swayed on her feet and he grabbed her around the waist, drawing her against him, causing her gown to slip from her shoulders and pool around his arms. He stood there, unable to move, her back pressed against him, his breathing nothing more than rough gasps as hunger exploded within him. He held her closer, inhaling the fragrance of woman and roses.

A soft whimper broke through his passion fogged brain and he realized how tightly he held her. Angered with himself, he pushed away, but kept his hands on her waist. "Oh God, Emma. I'm sorry. Did I hurt you?" Remorse tore at his chest, his voice a ragged whisper.

When she didn't answer, his heart sank. He'd hurt her, or worse, frightened her.

His hands trembled as he pulled the sleeves of her gown up over her shoulders and stepped back. "I'll leave you to finish." His voice shook with the effort it took to control himself.

Her gentle voice stopped him at the door.

"My corset…I can't unlace it."

He couldn't hold back the soft groan as he returned, loosened the laces, then turned and left the room.

This is going to be the longest night of my life.

CHAPTER
Eighteen

EMMA PACED AROUND HER OFFICE LIKE A CAGED TIGER, anxious and short tempered. Three days married and she was a bale of nerves, completely at a loss as to why she snapped like a shrew. And Ty, usually so calm and pleasant, had a short fuse as well.

Everyone around the ranch, even the one-eyed tomcat who claimed the barn as his home, avoided the newlyweds who were prone to snap with little or no provocation.

Although he spent the last three nights in her bed, he made no attempts to touch her. He always insisted she turn in first then came in, undressed and slipped under the covers. She woke to find him gone and hated to admit how much she enjoyed having him near. The sound of his gentle snores, the smell of him, the heat of him, all worked together to drive her to distraction. He promised to kiss her and touch her and yet he had done neither and she wondered why.

Never one to shirk a necessary task, she racked her brain for every tidbit of information Sarah and Mable gave her regarding marriage. Some she dismissed as foolish, other pieces tantalized her imagination and caused her body to react in ways she wasn't familiar with, yet intuitively understood it all came back to the man-woman thing she knew so little about.

She devoted the morning to figuring out a course of action, then clarity struck.

It was the problem.

The constant worry of when Ty would decide the time arrived to be husband and wife. Would he keep his word and not force her? Should she do something first? Was she ready for this next very important step? She pictured him lying in her bed, bare chest gleaming in the moonlight, visions of what lay beneath the covers haunted her dreams, made her body ache with a need she couldn't define.

With a deep breath for courage, she made up her mind. *It's time to stop this nonsense, and just get it over with.*

A plan began to form.

Ty closed the ledger after entering the last figures. The wedding, a stampede and unexpected bad weather delayed the start of the roundup so they needed to start tomorrow, regardless. But the thought of leaving Emma alone tore at his gut.

Mostly because of Walker.

He deemed the man was somehow involved in their string of bad luck with the cattle but lacked any kind of proof. With him gone, Emma would be unprotected, and there was no doubt in his mind she needed to be protected from the bastard whether she would admit it or not.

I couldn't bear it if something happened and I wasn't here.

Rafe's condition neither improved nor declined but still, she hesitated to leave him and finally decided not to go on the drive this time. A good and bad deal for Ty. Good because seeing the curve of her luscious backside in jeans would be continued torture. Bad because he believed she'd be vulnerable without him.

Getting married seemed like a good idea at the time but at this moment, he was a sexually frustrated, unhappily married man.

With a heavy exhale, he swiveled the chair and surveyed the expanse of yard visible through the window. The brilliant blue of a cloudless sky was offset by the faded red barn. Chickens pecked at the ground under the huge oak trees where the wedding celebration took place. He smiled, remembering how self-conscious she acted when it came time to dance with him in front of everyone. In spite of all her grit and determination, she was, at heart, very shy and he found that endearing.

His eyes drifted back to the chuck wagon in front of the barn where final preparations were in process. Everything would be ready to head out at first light but his insides twisted every time he thought about it. That three-week trip stretched like an eternity before him.

The hair on his neck prickled at the change in atmosphere. He sensed her presence behind him, but didn't turn around.

Neither spoke.

She puffed out a breath, but remained silent.

He turned to face her and stiffened. His mouth went dry as overwhelming desire blindsided him.

She wore the same moss green gown that drove him crazy enough to suggest marriage in the first place. His eyes briefly met hers, then slid down to her breasts, their luscious fullness accentuated by the hands clasped in front. The fabric of her gown fell away from a small waist to drape over feminine hips. Those curls he ached to touch, the tiny ribbon at the nape of her neck he yearned to pull free, all threatened to unhinge his resolve.

He clenched his fists for control, unable to speak.

Her cheeks glowed a bright red as his eyes made their way back up them.

"I, um, thought, um, since you are leaving out tomorrow we could, um, have an early dinner and go to bed, um, I mean retire early."

He could not remember ever seeing anyone blush the way she did; the color highlighting her eyes till they shone like precious gems.

He cleared this throat. "I, uh, thought I'd bunk with the men tonight so I wouldn't wake you when we left. We'll head out before daybreak."

Her face scrunched up and she nibbled her lower lip. "Oh."

Is that disappointment I see in her face? He scrambled to salvage his mistake. "But if you've got dinner planned…"

"I do, um, have plans…for dinner."

Her quick response and the ensuing smile put a hitch in his breathing as lust engulfed him. *Lord help me.*

"It'll be on the table in a few minutes if you want to wash up first."

She whirled and left the room, leaving him gasping for air and shifting to ease the tightness in his jeans he endured just being in the same room with her.

Ten minutes later, he entered the dining room to find his new wife seated at the table, a glass of wine in her hand.

He sat opposite her, noted his glass held a healthy drink as well and tasted it. "Is there something special we should toast?"

Crimson color flooded her face but her gaze didn't waver. "To us. Tonight."

He choked on his wine. "Tonight?"

She looked down at her plate, gulped down the rest of her wine and refilled the glass, sloshing some over the rim in the process. She drank half of it in one swallow and faced him, her voice edged with tension. "Dammit! I'm no good at this. I listened to what Sarah and Mable said, but hell, I can't remember anything. I don't know how to be seductive or whatever it is I need to be to get you in the mood. I've no idea what I should be doing. I thought I did, but…"

"In the mood?"

She flung her napkin on the table. "Yes. For us to…you know."

Lupe entered carrying platters of food which she placed in the center of the table. Evidently sensing the tension between them, she turned and left the room.

Alone again, Ty took a cautious sip of his wine, and looked at Emma. She sat ramrod straight, hands no doubt fisted in her lap as she waited for…what?

"Are you saying you want to…?"

"Yes. I'm tired of waiting and worrying when it's gonna happen. We need to just do it and get it over with."

He sat back in his chair, and stared. *What the hell? Talk about a mood breaker.*

"*Get it over with*? That's how you see it? Something to just get over with?"

She shot from her chair and paced beside the table, hands flailing in the air. "I don't know! Dammit! I don't know! And it's driving me crazy." She rounded the end of the table and stood in front of him, apprehension evident in her pinched expression. "*You* make me crazy!" Her hands floundered about as she ranted. "I think about the stuff Sarah told me and I want to know if what she said is true or hogwash. I have these…these feelings I don't know what to do about… now you're going to be gone for weeks and you said you were going to kiss me and touch me and you didn't, and you're so warm next to me, and I want to touch you and I don't know if I'm supposed to or not or what the hell is happening to me."

She waited, hands clenched at her sides, chest rapidly rising and falling as she fought to catch her breath.

He struggled for calm, released the grip he had on the fragile wineglass less he break it. The last thing he wanted to do was alarm her. "I didn't kiss you or touch you because I knew it would be a mistake."

She jerked back like he'd hit her.

"Not that kind of mistake, Em." He stood, reached for her, then dropped his hands. "The kind that would make it impossible for me to keep my word and not push. Because, after that first night, when I had to help you undress… I knew one kiss, one touch, would never be enough."

"It-it wouldn't?"

He shook his head.

She closed her eyes and gripped the sides of her head,

jostling delicate tendrils caressing her cheek, softening the strained features. "There's so much I don't know about this, this man-woman thing." She opened her eyes and met his. "I mean, I know what horses and cows do so I'm guessing it's similar."

Horses and cows? "Em…what horses and cows do is nothing like what happens between a man and a woman." He placed his hands on her arms and gently caressed up and down. "The…mechanics I guess are the same, but the feelings…" A tremble rippled through her at his touch. "The feelings enhance the experience."

"Sarah said it's… difficult …the first time."

"Is that what you're afraid of?"

She swallowed hard, and nodded.

"As far as I know, there's nothing to be done to … to ease that. I can just promise to be as gentle as I can." *And get it over with.*

Her smile was timid, trusting. "I know." She puffed out a long breath. "Have you, um, ever been with someone…like me?"

There is no one like you.

She backed away. "I'm sorry, I shouldn't've asked."

"No secrets, Em." He stuffed his hands in his pockets and blew out a breath. "Once. A long time ago. Before the war. We were engaged to be married." *She hated it, would never let me near her afterwards. Please God don't let it be that way again.*

She bobbed her head, eyes downcast. "At least one of us will know what to do."

H worked hard not to smile at her seriousness. "Shall we finish our dinner?"

She slanted her eyes toward him, and his heart stumbled. *Who says you don't know how to be seductive?*

"I don't think I can eat right now." She licked her lips. "I think I'll just…go upstairs and - and wait for you."

CHAPTER
Nineteen

Emma's knees shook so badly she had to grab the bedpost to keep from falling. Her body sizzled with a need she didn't understand as she recalled the feel of his hands on her skin, his warm breath on her cheek. *Is this the pleasure Sarah talked about or the pain?*

She sat on the edge of the bed and worked to get enough air in her lungs and heart rate to a more normal level. "Oh my stars in heaven. How will I ever get through this?" She walked to the wardrobe and pulled out her night clothes. Her sleeveless cotton gown, constructed like a chemise in deference to the hot summer nights, stopped just below the knees and had a deep scoop neckline accented with tiny rose colored bows.

"Thank goodness this one buttons in the front," she muttered as she quickly shed her clothes and pulled the gauzy garment over her head, pausing to glance at her reflection in the tall mirror.

"Oh my goodness!" The shift's low cut bodice revealed the top half of ample breasts, the hardened tips clearly visible through the thin fabric along with the dark triangle below her waist. "I may as well be naked!"

At first, it was shocking seeing herself in this new light, but on the heels of that thought raced another: *What will Ty think?*

By the time the question materialized, a soft knock on the door had her spinning around as he walked in.

She couldn't move if she wanted to.

Her body sizzled under the heat of his gaze as his eyes raked boldly over her. He zeroed in on the twin peaks pushing against the filmy fabric causing them to ache.

His gaze dropped lower. His nostrils flared as he sucked in a breath.

A strange tingling sensation enveloped her as molten heat pooled in her middle, provoking a gasp as the intense and unfamiliar emotions assailed her.

The soft click of the door closing behind him sounded like a thunderclap in the room. Slow and deliberate, eyes focused on hers, he moved forward, stopping an arms-length away. His chest rose and fell in rapid, uneven movements, his voice a husky whisper. "You are so beautiful."

He stepped closer, reached behind her neck and removed the ribbon holding her hair in check. His hands trembled as he ran calloused fingers through the burnished strands, pulling them to his face where he inhaled the intoxicating aroma. "I've been wanting to do this since the first time I saw you."

He cradled her face in his hands, leaned down and brushed her lips with his, softly, then, with a low groan, claimed them with a hungry, sensual kiss that left her clinging to him to keep from dropping into a heap on the floor.

He pulled back and looked at her. "I will try my best to go slow and easy." He closed his eyes and rested his forehead against hers, sucking in a deep gulp of air. "But I want you more than my next breath." He pushed back, slid his hands down her arms. "If I go too fast, do something you don't like, tell me and I'll try to stop." He paused. "But once we get to a certain point, there won't be any stopping."

She gripped his shirt front. "I know." Her breathing stumbled. "Sarah said if you know what you're doing, you'd show me my pleasure afterwards."

His slight smile made her stomach flutter.

"She said that did she?"

"Uh-huh. She said she was pretty sure you knew how."

"What else did she say?"

She ran her hands up his chest, clutching his shirt. "I don't remember." Her impatience grew to explosive levels. "Can you take this off, please?"

He sat on the edge of the bed and yanked off one boot then the other. Standing, he pulled his shirt over his head, sending a button or two flying.

"I don't know what's wrong with me," she whispered, hands splayed over his chest, fingers scraping through the tight curls. "I can't decide if I'm hot or cold; it's like I got this itch I can't scratch and I'm all jittery inside."

"It's desire, Red. The kind of thing a husband and wife should feel for each other."

She breathed in deep, soul drenching drafts. "It's like I need something but I don't know what it is."

"...I do."

He devoured her mouth. The hunger in his kiss

shattering her composure. He slid his hands down and pulled her against him.

She felt his hardness and molded herself to him, arms entwined around his neck, seeking…something.

He trailed kisses down her neck, her shoulder, bringing his hand up to cup one breast. She moaned low in her throat as he rubbed his thumb over the taunt nipple. Lowering his head, he pushed the thin fabric aside and took the dimpled peak in his mouth, sucking gently, then more firmly as she grasped his head and held him to her, a soft whimper escaping pursed lips.

He pulled back, brows drawn together in an agonized expression. "I want you to be sure, Emma. I don't know if I can stop if we go any further."

She clung to his shoulders. "I do want it, Ty. I want to be your wife. Show me what I need to do."

With a low growl, he ravished her mouth again, one hand behind her neck, the other kneading her swollen breast. Then, he lifted her in his arms and placed her gently on the bed, then lay down beside her. "…I hate knowing what comes next is going to hurt you." He ran a calloused finger down her neck, over her chest, pushing the gown a little lower. "I'll do what I can to make it…easier, but…"

Her breathing was uneven but she met his gaze with as much confidence as she could muster. "Sarah said it's kinda like the time she dared me to poke a stick in a hornets' nest."

His head jerked back and his eyes widened.

She thought he bit back a smile.

"A hornet's nest?"

She nodded. "She said it may be easy and it may be difficult. You just have to get it over with."

He lowered his head, took a breath.

"…Ty?"

He met her gaze. "Emma, telling a man to *get it over with* is not exactly what he wants to hear at this point."

She gnawed her lower lip. "I know I'm doing this all wrong, but the fact is, I want to know you…as a wife knows a husband. I know I probably won't enjoy it…but Sarah said I would the next time." She eased her arms around his neck. "I don't know what I need to say or do to, well, get you back in the mood, but, if you'll just tell me, I'll do it."

Those captivating eyes darkened to a slate gray as he looked at her, lips curling into a slow, sexy smile that made her insides go all fluttery and heat flash in her woman parts.

"All you need to do is smile at me, Red, and I'd be in the mood."

Her brows creased. "Really?"

"Really."

She licked her lips, saw his eyes rivet on her mouth then did her best to give him an enchanting smile. "Will this do?"

"It will."

His kiss was possessive, demanding, and left no doubt as to his mood.

His hand cupped her breast, teasing the taut bud with his thumb until she squirmed and arched toward him. Then, it slid lower, over her stomach which tightened at his touch, down her thigh to the edge of her gown.

His hand slipped under the translucent fabric, hovered near the cleft between her legs. She instinctively arched toward his hand. "Ty…"

His fingers grazed the dense curls, over the swollen nub that begged for his attention.

Startled by the touch, and the resulting sensations surging through her, she gasped, then bowed toward his drifting hand.

He pressed his palm down over her, sliding one calloused finger over the tight bud, retreated, and then slid again.

She struggled to take a breath as each stroke brought her untried passion to life.

Long fingers grazed her, then delved into the delicate softness making her writhe beneath him.

"Ty!"

His movements were slow and methodical, the gentle stroke of his hand sending currents of desire through her.

He stopped his intimate caressing to lift the edge of her gown. In one swift movement, she was naked. The hot look in his eyes stymied the impulse to cover herself.

Soft as a caress, stormy grey eyes slid over her. "You're perfect," he whispered. Then his hand seared a path down her body, over sensitive, swollen nipples, down her taunt abdomen to the swell of her hip. He lowered his head, suckled first one breast, then the other until she cried out again. He covered her mouth with a tender kiss, then stood, fumbled with his belt, and shucked his jeans and drawers.

She focused on his erection, eyes wide. "Oh my. Will that fit?"

"…Yes."

He lay down beside her, placed one on hand on her belly causing her stomach to contract, and he paused. His gaze traveled over her face, searched her eyes. A question shimmered in those smoldering depths along with a passion he made no effort to hide.

She experienced a moment of panic. *It's time. Can I do this?*

She pushed the anxiety aside and focused on what he did to her, body and soul.

She wanted this. She wanted him.

Compelled by her passion, she pushed up on one elbow and placed a timid kiss on his chin, his nose, then brushed his lips with hers, declaring without words she was his, wholly, completely.

He groaned, and took possession of her mouth in a devastating, soul-reaching massage. Raising his mouth from hers, he burned a path down her neck, across her shoulder, his feather-light kisses sending shockwaves through her.

One hand slid over her breast, its tip marble hard. He squeezed the beautifully formed globe, shaping and re-shaping it, rubbing the tight, rosy bud between his fingers.

Consumed by a burning desire, an aching need, she pushed his head toward the throbbing peak.

He took the dusky tip in his mouth, suckling hard and eliciting a tiny whimper. He moved to the other one, nipping it with his teeth, then laved it with his tongue.

Fingers fisted in his hair, she held him to her breast as she squirmed beside him.

His hand slid down her body and resumed its rhythmic ministrations to her entrance as he suckled harder, making it difficult to focus on anything except the exquisite chaos he created within her.

Her nails dug into his back as she pushed against the fingers sweeping over and into her womanhood, unable to get close enough, recognizing something building, growing inside her until she exploded in a fiery downpour of sensations so intense she cried out in sweet agony. "Ty!"

He poised over her, face contorted as he struggled for control. "I'm sorry." His raspy voice floated over hypersensitive nerve endings, barely registering over the flood of reactions surging through her body as it convulsed and jerked in an eruption of ecstasy like nothing she'd ever known.

She had no time to prepare for what was about to happen before it did.

He thrust hard, backed off, pressed again, filling her, pushing against her insides like an invading army.

Agonizing pain, unlike anything she had ever felt, like being ripped in two from the inside, racked her body. She cried out, shoved against his shoulders in a futile defense but he persisted until he lay buried deep inside her.

She never let anyone see her cry, and tried desperately to stop the tears cascading from tightly clenched eyes. More even than her own discomfort at such an emotional reaction, she understood they would hurt him, and didn't want to do so, but couldn't stop.

"I'm so sorry. I'm so sorry." He pressed his lips to her forehead, hands braced on either side of her head to keep his bulk off her as he stiffened, unmoving, and breathing hard.

She didn't know how long it was before his gruff voice again penetrated the veil of pain. "Oh God, Em...I need to finish this."

Tears clouded her vision, and words wouldn't come so she nodded. *I never expected it to be like this. Just get it over with!*

He pulled back, pushed forward slowly. Again. And again, scraping over the raw flesh. She clamped her jaw to keep from crying out, barely breathing, so tense a cramp formed in her back.

Sarah said it wouldn't last. Sarah said it wouldn't last. She repeated the mantra over and over as she gripped the bed covers and waited for it to end.

Then, to her utter amazement, the pain dissipated. Tenderness remained, but the insufferable agony was gone, replaced by something altogether new and exciting. The grazing of his chest hair over her nipples made them pucker and ache. The slide of his sweat-coated body against hers re-kindled the fire she thought doused.

He filled her, completed her. She pulsed and tingled with each slow thrust he made; flesh against flesh, man against woman.

She forced her eyes open and looked at Ty, whose own eyes were clinched tight as he carefully moved in and out, muscles tense and trembling.

She slid her arms around his waist, hands sweeping up and down his back as she slowly relaxed and opened herself to him. Her fingers dug into the tight muscles as another wave of pleasure threatened to overtake her.

He opened his eyes, found her gaze on him, saw the passion growing there, and with a strangled exclamation, drove into her again, each thrust coming harder and faster until she shuddered, then convulsed around him as he reached the brink himself, and plummeted over the edge.

It was over with.

CHAPTER
Twenty

Ty SAVORED THE WARMTH OF THE WOMAN CRADLED against him, her head nestled in the hollow between his shoulder and neck. He fingered the burnished curls lying against her back, marveling at the silky softness, then slid his hand down over her waist to rest on her hip.

She sighed and shifted against him producing a quick jolt of renewed desire as her knee slid up and down his thigh, the intimacy of the moment wrapping around his heart like a warm blanket.

She had yet to say anything about *it* which bothered him more than he wanted to admit. Visions of Jenni's tearful rejection following their hasty coupling danced in his head causing his own anxiety to rise.

How will Emma feel about me...us when she wakes up? Knowing he hurt her filled him with regret. Her tear-stained face was forever imbedded in his memory. But he also knew she reached her pleasure. Twice. Therefore, he allowed himself a small sliver of hope.

He turned his head toward the open window. Darkness had fallen and a near-full moon bathed the room in a vaporous light. Dawn would come much too early to suit him.

"It wasn't too bad."

Her quiet voice startled him and he couldn't stop the light flinch at her words. *Well, that ranks right up there with let's-just-get-it-over-with on the mood killer list.*

"The pain, I mean. It wasn't too bad."

His jaw clenched, relaxed. "It made you cry. A lot."

Her breath was feather soft on his skin. "I'm not crying now." She ran her fingers through the tight curls on his chest. "Sarah said we might have to wait before, well, you know."

His hand moved up to her waist, then back down to skim that luscious behind. "Yeah, I know."

"Why did you call me Red? My hair isn't red."

The quick change of topic confused him a moment. "When the sun hits it just right, it has these fiery streaks in it."

Her hand slid a little lower. "But it's not red."

He lost his train of thought when her finger circled his belly button and he fought to remember what he wanted to say. "Did it bother you? To be called Red?"

"Not the way you said it."

His attention focused. "How did I say it?"

He felt it on his chest when she chewed her lip. *Why do I find that nibble thing so damn sexy?*

"It's hard to describe. You have such a nice voice." Her fingers continued to circle. "Sometimes it changes and… makes me feel, well, all funny inside." She paused. "Like when you look at me a certain way."

Her hand stilled when his body responded with a quick twitch.

She raised up and looked at him, then cut her eyes toward the evidence of his arousal pushing against the light cotton sheet.

It twitched again.

Her voice an awestruck whisper, she looked at him. "Can I touch it?"

He spoke with quiet emphasis. "I don't think that's a good idea right now."

Raising one fine, arched brow, she protested. "Why not? We're married now. And you touched me."

He closed his eyes, chose his words carefully, and explained to his innocent wife why it wasn't such a good idea at this point in time.

"Oh. I see."

The way her expression changed with her thoughts fascinated him.

"You're going to be gone a while."

"Yeah."

She bit her lip. "We don't have much time together."

And I'll be hell to live with on the trail. "I know."

"You probably want to sleep."

He grinned. "Sleep is overrated with a beautiful, naked woman in your bed." *Shit! She may not like that kinda talk.*

Amusement flickered in the eyes meeting his. "Or a handsome man."

His body ignored all his efforts at control and twitched again.

She ducked her head, then looked at him from the corner of her eye. "Is that okay to say?"

"Hell, yeah." *She thinks I'm handsome.*

She shrugged, and one coppery curl wrapped around a nipple.

His groin tightened more and his mouth envied that curl.

"Not very ladylike."

"Don't ever hold back from me, Red. Good, bad or otherwise, if you have something to say, say it."

She looked at him intently as though trying to ascertain if he were serious or not.

"I…I liked what…we did."

Thank you, God.

She cut her eyes to his rapidly growing erection. "Sarah said there are…other ways to…find pleasure."

When she turned her head and cut those amazing green orbs toward him, his heart thundered. *Damn! She has no idea of how sexy that look is!*

"Do you…happen to, um, know what she meant?"

Sarah's my new best friend. "Did she…give you any specifics?"

"Not really."

Her fingers dipped a little lower.

"She said I should just let you teach me what to do."

So he did.

Emma woke before the first rays of sun peaked in her bedroom window, dismayed to find herself alone. She stretched, relishing the slide of cotton sheets over bare skin, remembering how Ty's fingers did the same thing last night. She was blissfully happy and fully alive for the first time in her life. *I*

am liking this man-woman thing!

Before the thought completed, she jerked up in bed. He would be leaving this morning. For three weeks! Maybe longer. And he didn't wake her before he left.

She jumped from the bed and grabbed her robe from the chair. Tying the sash, she walked to the window and looked out in time to see Ty strolling across the yard to the barn.

He stopped when he reached the door, paused, and then turned as though he knew she watched.

She waved, and he nodded before entering the barn. She turned and scrambled around for clothes, choosing a simple muslin gown and chemise. In record time, she stood in the kitchen, thankful Lupe was occupied elsewhere, and grabbed a cup of hot coffee and a biscuit from the warming shelf on the oven. A quick gulp and a bite and she headed out the door in time to see Ty, Leo and three other hands standing with their horses near the barn.

She started in their direction, an equal mixture of anticipation and dread slowing her step. *What will he think of me this morning?* She cursed the heat coursing up her neck, aware it was an outward manifestation of what transpired between them.

A sure sign not be missed by Ty. Or the ranch hands with him.

Stiffening her back, she strode forward. *I'm a married woman now with no cause to be ashamed.*

When he turned and spotted her coming toward him his slow, sexy smile turned her insides to mush.

With pulse-pounding certainty, it hit her. She was hopelessly in love. The realization made her stumble, and he instinctively grabbed her to him, setting off an explosion of desire.

"If you think I'm letting you go without saying good-bye," she whispered, one hand resting on his chest, "you've got another think coming." She hoped she did not sound as breathless as she felt being this close to him as memories of last night spun around in her head.

She pulled back a step and met his probing gaze. Her cheeks burned in remembrance and she knew by the look in his eyes, he remembered as well.

"You were sleeping so soundly, I didn't want to wake you." He lowered his voice to a soft whisper, "because I knew I couldn't leave you if I did."

Ripples of need rolled over her as she met his heated look with one of her own. "It's going to be a long three weeks."

"I know."

Neither spoke, for there was a deeper significance to the visual exchange.

She had a burning desire, an aching need to kiss him. Her voice faded to a hushed whisper as she placed her hands on his face and drew him to her. "I love you, Tyler Roundtree. Hurry back to me."

And then she kissed him, a lingering, savoring-every-second kind of kiss.

In front of the men.

He tensed, then enveloped her in his embrace, softly, gently, as he responded to her actions while still allowing her to control the kiss.

She wrapped her arms around his neck, pressing against him as she lost herself in the tenderness of the moment.

At last, they parted a few inches. Embarrassed at her

wanton behavior, but nonetheless relishing the newfound freedom it brought, she met Ty's impassioned gaze.

His arms trembled as he brushed a gentle kiss across her forehead, hot breath fanning her cheek as he groused, "You're killing me, Red."

She rested her hand on his chest, the rapid thump of his heart matching her own. "Well, I'm new at this stuff myself, but I'm pretty sure it's mutual."

At last, sanity returned and she stepped from his embrace, cutting a quick glance toward the ranch hands, surprised to see they had ambled off a short distance, allowing them some privacy.

Ty turned toward Diablo, then back to her. He ran a gloved finger down her cheek. "I'll be home as soon as I can."

Then he mounted and they rode away.

Once they were out of site, reality hit.

He never said he loved me.

CHAPTER
Twenty-One

T y avoided looking at the men, Leo in particular, as they road west toward the waiting herd, his mind occupied by two astounding thoughts: *She kissed me in front the men. She loves me.*

He didn't think she even realized she spoke out loud. But he didn't say it back. Did he love her? Did he even know what love was? He kicked Diablo into a canter, distancing himself from the others, his mind racing, looking for answers to the questions swirling around his head.

He was thrilled with her response to his love making. Shy at first, she quickly wanted to know more, explore more and just the memory of her exploration had him ready to explode.

An extremely passionate woman, it thrilled him to be the one to bring it out in her. On the heels of that thought came the questions: Would it have been the same if she married anyone? Leo maybe? Or even Walker?

One minute he believed he was the only reason, the next, he wondered. *How could such a beautiful, passionate woman, remain untouched?* She had a quick temper, sure but just as quickly, it passed. Strong and independent, she possessed a soft, vulnerable side that brought out the protector in him.

He thought over the last few weeks and had to admit to seeing a gradual but definite change in her. Standoffish at first, she now sought him out to discuss the ranch, or to just take a ride with her. She worked as hard as any man and yet maintained her femininity. Rafe told him she rarely wore dresses… until Ty came along. She appeared more at ease around him and smiled when she saw him.

She loves me.

He told her up front he wasn't sure about love and she accepted his answer. He desired her without question but would desire be enough to keep their marriage a happy one?

Thoughts of her kisses, her body…there was no way in hell he would survive the long, drawn out weeks ahead without hurting someone.

He reached the edge of the herd in a foul mood at best, and the men gave him a wide berth.

"Leo, you and the boys split up right and left flank." Ty's curt voice brooked no discussion. "I'll run drag a while."

The most hated part of the drive. Nothing but dust, hard-headed mavericks and cow shit.

A perfect complement to his mood.

Emma sat talking with her father, amazed at how much better he appeared to be doing over the last few days. He didn't cough quite as much and the awful wheezing sound when he breathed lessened. Tonight, he even ate most of his supper.

"You look a lot better today, Papa. And you ate most of your supper tonight."

"Yeah, still can't fight off a flea, though."

His reference to his weakened state reminded her of Doc's parting words earlier today. *"He's better but he ain't out of the woods yet. He's weak as a kitten and the least infection could do him in."*

"Well, you just do like Doc says and you'll be up and about in no time."

He rolled his head from side to side. "I get tired of laying here like a baby all day. I like it when Ty comes in and helps me to a chair."

"He's a good man."

"Yes, he is. You done good marrying him. What time did they head out? I never heard 'em."

"About sunup. Are probably a little south of the Oakman place by now providing they didn't experience any troubles."

"Surprised you didn't go. Especially since your new husband did."

Heat rushed to her cheeks and she avoided looking at him. "Well, I thought he could handle things without me."

"Meaning you thought you needed to be here."

"Meaning I wanted to be here."

Rafe looked at her, his pale blue eyes filled with regret. "I should'a done better by you, Girl." He shook his head slowly. "I meant well, but…"

She placed her hand over his. "I know, Papa. I know." And suddenly, she did know. She understood his need to see her married, to be happy. And because she had Ty, she was.

He stared for a long moment. "A father should always tell his daughter how proud he is and that he loves her." His lips trembled and he took a long breath. "I never done that. But I am proud, Girl. No father could ever be prouder."

She bit her lip for control, but still her eyes filled with tears. "Thank you, Papa." She bent over and kissed his weathered cheek. "I love you. More than I can say."

His eyes slid shut. "I love you, too, Emma-girl."

She sat there until she decided he slept soundly, then kissed his forehead, picked up the food tray, and headed for the kitchen.

"Good evening, Señ*ora* Roundtree."

Emma avoided Lupe's gaze as she placed the tray on the table. "What happened to Emma?"

Amusement flickered in her doe-like eyes. "You are a married woman now. And judging by the smile you wore most of the day, I'd say a very happy one."

Emma silently fumbled with the contents of the tray.

"I am sorry. I have embarrassed you." Lupe placed her soft hands on Emma's. "I am just so happy to see such a beautiful smile on your face."

"Yes, well, um, marriage is not so bad."

Lupe's gentle laugh rippled through the warm kitchen. "No, it is not." Dusting her hands on her apron, she picked up the tray. "*Señor* Rafe ate very well tonight. That is good." She placed it on the counter near the sink. "Shall I fix a plate for you?"

"No thank you. I'm not hungry at the moment. Why don't you go ahead and go home to José. I'll clean up in here."

"The house is lonesome without Señor Ty, no?"

Emma picked up a plate, set it back down. "Yes. It is."

Lupe nodded and took off her apron. "I will see you in the morning, Señora."

An hour later, Emma paced from the bed to the window and back again, too tense to even consider sleep. The moon edged up over the horizon when she gave up any pretense of slumber. Ty was out there somewhere. Was he thinking about her? Did he know how it distressed her not to go with them or how she longed to have him beside her, fanning the flames of desire that even now raced through her?

With a frustrated groan, she left the house and headed for the barn. She needed a ride to cool her too warm body.

By the time she reached her special place by the creek, the moon was high enough to fill the valley with light.

She looped the reins over a branch and lay down, eyes fixed on the twinkling stars above. "Have you ever seen a sky so beautiful, Midnight?"

The mare silently munched grass.

"I wonder if Ty is looking at these same stars."

A soft snort indicated her companion's lack of interest in conversation.

"God, I can't believe how much I miss him and it's only been one day!" She rolled her head and closed her eyes. "I wish Ty was here now."

"He is."

She jerked upright and stood at the sound of his voice. "Ty! What are you doing here? Is everything all right? Did something happen?"

He clutched Diablo's reins in his hand and cleared his throat. "The boys told me to get the hell away from them till I could act human again."

"I don't understand."

He didn't explain. "I was headed home when I saw you riding hell bent for leather. I thought something happened to Rafe."

"I couldn't sleep."

"Me neither." He looped the reins over a limb away from Midnight and faced her, his gaze intense. "I couldn't get you out of my mind."

Tingles of awareness burst through her at his soft-spoken words, her long dormant sexuality jumping to life. "Really?"

He slowly nodded. "I had to see you."

She took a tentative step toward him. "I haven't stopped thinking about last night."

"Me neither."

She glanced around, nibbled her lower lip and looked at him from the corner of her eye. "We're alone here."

He pulled her roughly to him. "Damnit, Red," he whispered. "When you look at me like that, I can't think straight." He crushed his mouth to hers in a raw act of possession, the urgency of his need fused with her own.

Her lips burned in the aftermath of his passionate demonstration and she reveled in it. Giving herself freely to the hunger of his kisses, she met each thrust of his tongue with one of her own, communicating her own need in the most primal way.

He pulled back and the blazing desire reflected in those stormy pools turned her knees to butter.

He gulped air. "Are you sure you can handle this tonight?"

She yanked at the buckle of his gun belt. "I'm sure." It dropped to the ground with a heavy thud.

"This button drives me crazy," he whispered as he opened the top button of her shirt, exposing ample cleavage over the tight fitting chemise she wore underneath. He bent his head and trailed wet, open-mouthed kisses across the exposed flesh, the pebbly tips hardening, pressing against the fabric.

She moaned and arched toward him, relishing the feel of his lips on her over-heated skin.

He pulled the shirt from her pants and yanked it open, sliding it off her shoulders, followed by her chemise, leaving her upper body bare. He stood back and looked at her, his gaze hot and approving.

He went to Diablo, pulled the blanket from the back of the saddle and spread it on the ground beside her. Reaching behind her neck, he pulled the ever-present ribbon loose and let her hair fall free. He raked his fingers through the chestnut curls, then pulled her to him again.

His kiss was surprisingly tender but still had her senses reeling.

He lowered her gently to the ground, and removed her boots, stopping to gaze at her with open want. He jerked his shirt over his head then sat down beside her and removed his boots. He joined her on the rough blanket, one hand cupping her breast, his thumb rubbing the hardened peak as he kissed the hollow at the base of her throat.

Her hands roamed his body, memorizing each line and curve as they slid over the muscled planes. She reached out to finger the curls on his chest, raking her nails across his tight nipples, enjoying the quick intake of breath that said he liked it. She pushed up and licked one tight nub, then the other before nipping at the tiny protrusion.

He groaned and rolled on his back, pulling her atop him, her hair forming a dark curtain on either side of his head. His hands gripped her hips, pressing her against the evidence of his need.

She lowered her head and caressed his lips with hers, mimicking movements learned from him, her tongue lightly tracing the fullness before delving inside to taste the richness there.

He pressed her cleft tighter against him, and then with soft growl, he towered over her, his eyes devouring her. Without a word, he worked at the buttons of her jeans, sliding them past her hips, down her legs.

Her thoughts scattered to the four winds as his hands and lips continued their hungry exploration of her body, scorching a trail down her neck, across her taut abdomen, and then lower, to the burning apex in the middle, his expert touch sending her to even higher levels of ecstasy. And then his mouth was on her, his tongue tracing the path his fingers took. All thought left. Nothing remained except the exquisite torture his mouth inflicted on her. Long fingers fisted in his hair as she clung to him, soft whimpers mixing with the sounds of the night as she writhed beneath his sensual assault.

When he stopped, she cried out in dismay. "Ty, please!"

He struggled to rid himself of his jeans. "Hang on, Red."

And then he lay beside her again, his hand stoking the fire raging within her, as his lips explored the creamy flesh of her neck, her breasts.

Each took the time to explore the other, to arouse and give pleasure before his body moved to cover hers and she welcomed him inside.

They moved in perfect harmony, the tempo binding their bodies together, soaring higher and higher until they crested the brink as one in an exhilarating burst of pleasure that left them crying out, spent and breathless.

CHAPTER
Twenty-Two

SHE LAY CURLED AGAINST HIS SWEAT-COATED BODY, AND an amazing sense of contentment surrounded him. He fingered the curls lying over her shoulder, their softness contrasting sharply with his hard, calloused hand.

She sighed and her warm breath caressed his chest. All doubts from earlier disappeared. She was his. His alone. He tightened his hold and she responded by pressing herself against him, hand splayed over his heart, one leg laying over his.

He wanted to ask her how it felt to be in love, but even as the thought materialized he knew the answer.

It felt like now. Under the stars, with her in his arms, her goodness and sweetness surrounding him. *Is this love? Or just the afterglow of making love to a passionate woman. Several times. In one night.*

"...Ty?"

Her soft question broke into his revelry. "Umm?"

She seemed to like the hair on his chest because she kept running her fingers through it. Who was he to deny her something she enjoyed?

"I meant what I said when you left earlier."

He flinched, suddenly not ready for this conversation.

She raised up on her elbow to look at him, those glorious waves dropping over her shoulder to tickle his chest.

"I do love you. I think I loved you the first time I saw you in Ft. Worth. Don't ask me how it happened, because I don't know."

"Ft. Worth?" His eyes squinted and his brow creased.

She ducked her head. "I ran into you…literally, outside the El Paso Hotel back in April."

His head rocked back a little. "That was you?" His brows drew together. "A bonnet covered your hair and I barely saw your face."

She nodded. "I talked to the cattle buyer, then met with Mr. Ralston about the Herefords. I was on my way to the mercantile and ran into you." She paused for a heartbeat. "You were in my dreams every night for two weeks." A light shrug had her hair tickling his chest. "When I saw you in my office, I nearly passed out."

He nodded. "I thought you looked funny but couldn't figure out why."

She smiled. "You were the problem, but a good one."

"You don't know me…who I really am, what I've done."

"I know you are a good and honest man. You treat my father with dignity and respect. And you treat me like an equal, not someone to be tolerated or patronized. And you're patient with me when I don't understand things. Nothing else matters."

He opened his mouth to say…something, but a finger to his lips stopped him.

She paused as though choosing her words. "You told me to always say what I thought, not to hold back and that's what I did. Well, I have a tendency to do so anyway, but this whole man-woman-married thing is different."

She took a deep breath and fixed those captivating eyes on his. "I am discovering a lot of things I never knew before, and, well, I like it."

Her little half smile was so damn sexy his heart skipped and stuttered.

"I know things are different for a man."

He teased a bit to lighten the mood. "Sarah tell you that, too?"

She shook her head. "Mable. She said a man has to work up to being in love." She lowered her head, then raised it to meet his gaze. "I know you don't love me, but I think you care for me, and that's enough for now. Maybe…one day something will change, but for now I'm happy."

He didn't know what to say, was saved from ruining the moment by saying the wrong thing when she bent down and placed a timid kiss on his lips.

"How long will it take you to get back to the herd?"

"Diablo's had a good rest," *Unlike his master*, "so an hour or so tops."

A distant rumble of thunder had her looking to the west. "Another storm on the way." She looked down at him and smiled. "Think there's time…?"

He didn't think he had another round in him since the last one nearly gave him a heart attack. And then she straddled him and he discovered he was good to go.

Sometime later, Emma stood beside him as he checked the cinch and secured the bedroll back behind his saddle. The wind had picked up, and the stars so visible earlier were now obscured by clouds. "I'll ride with you back to the house."

She shook her head. "Don't be silly. The storm is probably going to catch you as it is. You should've left before now."

He turned around and his breath caught at the beauty in front of him. Her hair, mussed from their busy night, hung loose around her shoulders. Her shirt now lacked a couple of buttons thanks to his hurried attempt at undressing her and that ample bosom beckoned.

He grinned. "Well, as I recall, I was about to leave when my wife delayed me."

Even in the muted light, he saw the color fill her cheeks. "You complaining?"

"Hell no." He pulled her to him and she flattened her hands on his chest. "But I'd feel better if I knew you were safe at home."

"I'll be fine, don't worry. Won't be the first time I got caught in the rain." She stepped back from his embrace. "Got your knife handy?"

"My pocket. Why?"

She held out her hand. "Let me borrow it."

He pulled the knife and opened it, passing it to her.

She reached behind her head and pulled a thick strand of curls free, then sliced it off.

"What the hell are you doing?"

She handed him the knife, looped the strand around itself in a single knot and placed it in his other hand, closing his fingers around it. "Something to help you remember me by while you're gone."

A stunning sensation settled in the pit of his stomach. "There is no way in hell I'd ever forget you, Red." He kissed the length of hair and placed it in his breast pocket. "None at all."

He pulled her to him and kissed her, letting his actions convey what he could not. Stepping away from her was one of the hardest things he'd ever had to do as he grabbed up the reins and mounted. "I'll send you a telegram when I get to Ft. Worth and another when I am headed home."

Home. Just saying the word made him smile.

She stuffed her hands in her pockets. "The storm's gonna catch you for sure."

It surprised him to realize he was a little disappointed she didn't say she loved him again.

"I love you, Ty."

And then she did.

"Please be careful."

His heart rolled over in his chest.

He dismounted and walked to where she stood, a questioning look on her face.

"I've never been in love so I don't rightly know what it feels like." He took a steadying breath. "But I know the thought of not having you in my life is unbearable. I know you can smile at me and the world is perfect. I know I look forward to having you get mad at me just so I can see the fire in your eyes and then make up afterwards."

"Oh, Ty."

His voice was whisper soft as he continued. "If that's what it means to be in love…"

She blessed him with a teary-eyed smile. "I'm a lucky

woman, indeed."

Another roll of thunder asserted he would be soon be drenched. "We'll discuss this more when I get home." He gave her a quick kiss, then remounted and headed toward the herd, filled with a unique happiness he had never before experienced.

I think I'm in love.

By the time he neared the herd, the rain slacked off to a light shower from the torrential downpour he battled since shortly after leaving Emma. He estimated the herd to be maybe a mile up ahead, trailing parallel to the creek. The banks along this stretch were steep and they would stay well away from it. And after this much rain, flash floods were a real possibility. When he picked out the sounds of bawling cattle over the waning storm, he knew was close.

He heard the sharp retort of a gunshot a split second before a bullet ripped into his thigh. "Sonofabitch!" He ducked low over the horse's back and urged him forward. Another bullet tore into his shoulder, almost knocking him from the saddle. "Shit!" He estimated the gunman to be somewhere ahead and to the left of him, hidden by the dense foliage surrounding the creek. He pulled hard on the reins and sent his mount toward the semi-shelter of the trees. The next shot whistled by his ear, and then he was among the trees, reaching for his rifle, but unable to make his hand work.

Diablo stamped and side-stepped away from the noisy, rising waters.

"Easy boy, easy." He tried to calm the skittish horse

without much luck. Another shot dug into the tree behind him. "Where the hell is he!" He tried again to reach for his rifle but his arm was useless. He grabbed for his pistol with his good hand as the next shot came, grazing across his forehead, sending him over the bank into the now raging river. He inhaled sharply as the chilly water hit him, sucking him under. The pain of his injuries, momentarily forgotten, he struggled against the fast-moving current to get his head above water. Ears ringing, lungs burning, he at last broke the surface and pulled in air, flailing his good arm about looking for something – anything – to hold on to. A limb tickled his fingers and he grabbed for it just as something hard – his first thought was an uprooted tree — slammed against his head, pushing him back under the murky depths.

Stunned, he lost his hold on the limb as the water swept him downstream. His ears rang and his head hurt like a sonofabitch as he struggled to stay afloat. His fingers touched wood and he grabbed on, barely getting his face out of the water as darkness threatened to consume him. Weakened from his injuries and the struggle, he could only hold on and pray he didn't pass out and drown as the flood carried him downstream.

"I love you, Red," he whispered as darkness overtook him.

CHAPTER
Twenty-Three

EMMA AWOKE WITH A START, HEART POUNDING, AS thunder rolled and lightening flashed outside the window. She reached for Ty only to remember he was out there somewhere in the storm.

An unexpected sense of panic overwhelmed her. Throwing off the covers, she hurried to the window and looked out, expecting to see what caused her unease. The storm raged on as heavy sheets of rain pounded the ground, and gusty winds whipped limbs of the old oak trees around like blades of grass. She took a steadying breath. "It's just the storm."

Impending doom weighted her movements as she dressed and hurried downstairs. After checking on her father who slept soundly, she trudged to the kitchen, in dire need of strong coffee.

Edginess made it difficult to focus as she paced and

waited for the brew to finish. The first sip burned her lips and tongue and she welcomed the bitter taste as it slid down her throat. The hands wrapped around the mug trembled as she took another drink, savoring the rush of calm the heady liquid provided as it raced through her veins.

Ready to tackle yesterday's paperwork, she headed to the office. A drudge to some, she actually loved the mundane task of record keeping. Delving into the inner workings of the ranch, her ranch, gave her a great sense of pride. Today, it kept her from thinking about the gloom surrounding her and Ty being caught up the storm.

Lost in her work, time flew until Lupe's soft voice brought her back to the present.

"Señor*a*, do you wish me to take Señor Rafe's breakfast to him?"

Emma glanced up then to the clock on the mantel. *Eight o'clock?* She pushed back from the desk. "I'm sorry. I didn't realize it was so late. I'll be right there."

A few minutes later, she sat on the edge of the bed and watched her father eat slowly, the sense of dread stronger now than when she first woke.

"Some storm we had last night," he said between bites of scrambled eggs and bacon.

"Yeah, woke me about five. Couldn't get back to sleep so came down and did paperwork." She rubbed her arms, trying to ward off a chill that had nothing to do with the weather.

"What's bothering you, girl?"

"It's nothing, Papa. Just wondering how the drive is going, is all."

"They should be well south the Oakman place if the weather didn't stop 'em."

She nodded. "Ty said they made good time."

"How do you know?" he asked with a smile, "you in to mind-reading?"

Cheeks on fire, she didn't look at him. "Well, um, I took a ride last night down to that pretty spot beside the creek, the one with the big oaks on the East bank and met him there." She jumped up and headed for the door. "Lupe will be back later for the tray. I need to check on things outside; make sure the storm didn't do any damage."

She didn't miss the smile on her father's face as she whirled and walked out.

Thankfully, the storm caused no major damage around the ranch grounds. Some broken limbs and mud being the primary issues. She spent the rest of the day tending to chores, cleaning up debris, and trying to shake the uneasiness plaguing her.

By late afternoon, exhausted and covered in mud, thoughts of a hot bath and some quiet time to think were uppermost in her mind.

Movement in her peripheral vison drew her gaze westward. Two riders approached, one holding the reins of another horse.

Diablo.

Emma grabbed the porch post as her knees threatened to fold, the sense of dread crashing down on her.

Henry Oakman dismounted, and handed the reins to Wally Kincaid who sat with his head bowed.

She watched him walk up the steps, read what he was going to say in the pained expression on his face, and shook her head. "No," she whispered, "no."

Henry took her arm and pulled her toward the front

door, speaking to Wally over his shoulder. "Get him to the barn and get his wound taken care of."

"Wound? What wound?" She turned toward the young man.

"Come inside, Emma," said Henry kindly, "we need to talk."

"What wound, Henry?" She swallowed hard and whispered. "Where's Ty? What's happened?" She bit her lip until it throbbed like her pulse.

He didn't answer as he led the way down the hall to Rafe's room. "I don't want to do this twice."

Rafe looked up when they entered, the smile dying on his face. "Emma…what's going on?"

"I-I don't know." She looked at Henry.

He threw his hat toward the bed, pushing Emma in the chair beside it, and took a deep breath. "Wally came to the ranch this morning. Said one of the hands found Ty's horse hobbling along near the rear of the herd. There was blood on the saddle and a wound on his flank." He paused and looked at Rafe, then Emma. "It looks like maybe a bullet grazed him."

"A bullet!" Emma jumped from her chair. "Is he hurt? Where the hell is he?"

Henry faced her, his eyes filled with compassion and sorrow. "I'm so sorry, Emma."

"S-sorry? What do you mean, you're sorry?" Her voice rose several degrees and she grabbed his arm. "Where is he?"

"They looked for hours…there was no trace of him."

Rafe's stern voice commanded attention. "What the hell happened, Henry?"

"I don't honestly know, Rafe. When Wally got to the ranch, he said they couldn't find him and asked me to send some boys to help search." He looked back and forth between father and daughter. "We searched for two miles with no sign of him."

Panic welled up inside her. "And you just gave up!"

"There was no sign of him, Emma. Nothing. We went up and down both sides of the creek for over two miles. The flash flood last night…" Henry didn't finish his sentence. He didn't need to.

If Ty was wounded and ended up in the water…she clamped down on the thought, refusing to consider it. *He's alive. I know he is.*

"You said Diablo had a bullet wound…what makes you think that?" She kept her voice steady, despite the fear crushing her heart.

"Wally said he thought he heard a shot. He dismissed it at first, thinking it was the storm, then he heard another." Henry took a breath. "He headed for the sound and found the horse." He paused a moment. "And he found Ty's colt near the bank."

"And no sign of Ty?"

"No. He looked, called out for him. When he got no answer, he went back to camp and roused the others. They started looking and sent a rider to my place for help. We spent the next four hours looking for him."

Henry grabbed her arm as she turned for the door. "Where are you going?"

She jerked free. "To find my husband."

"Emma, he –"

"No! He's not dead! He's not." She bit her lip, fought for control. "I'd know if he was." She looked at her friend, then her father. "My heart would know."

An hour later, she stood beside Midnight, stowing provisions in her saddle bags.

"Emma, be reasonable." Henry's agitated voice showed his concern. "You can't go off alone like this. Hell, it's going to be dark before you get there. Give me time to get some men to go with you."

She checked the saddle of the extra horse she would take. One way or another, she would bring Ty home.

"He's out there and most likely hurt. I can't wait any longer." She patted the horse's head and turned back to her own mount. Lupe stood on the porch, a rag-wrapped package in her hand. "Take care of Papa for me, please."

"There are biscuits and ham in here along with some bacon." She nodded toward another package José held. "There is medicine and other provisions in there."

Emma placed the packs in the extra saddle bags before mounting her horse.

Wally rode up on a fresh mount. "I'll show you where we found his horse, Ma'am."

She nodded, turned west at a gallop.

I'm coming, Ty. I'm coming.

CHAPTER
Twenty-Four

I T TOOK OVER TWO HOURS OF HARD RIDING TO REACH THE spot Wally sought. "I found his horse over there," he pointed ahead and to the left, "by that big cypress tree. "Soon as I did, I started looking for him. It was still sprinkling some and dark. The water was near to the top of the bank." His voice lowered to a soft whisper. "I called out to him, but…"

Emma dismounted and walked to the edge of the creek, slipping in the mud as she stepped over a fallen tree to study the swirling waters below. "Still pretty high. Probably won't be normal until tomorrow or the next day."

She paced around the area, noting all the boot prints and hoof prints, saw where the water had crested the bank into the surrounding brush. "What about the gunshots? Henry said it looked like a bullet grazed Diablo."

He nodded. "I was on night watch. Maybe five or so when I thought I heard a gunshot. The storm had passed us but I still heard some thunder so I wasn't sure. When I heard it again, I knew it was a shot."

She stood beside a tall pine, trying to decide what to do next when she saw a bullet hole in the tree. No mistaking it. The bark was splintered by the impact. Her heart jumped. The obvious question of who would shoot Ty was overshadowed by the *why*.

I have to find him!

"Ok. You go on back to the herd. I'll take it from here."

Wally shifted in the saddle. "No, ma'am. I can't do that."

She hesitated, then nodded, thankful for the company. "Tell me who looked where and we'll go from there."

Each taking a side, they trudged on foot along the edge of the creek, the brush making it too hard to traverse on horseback. They searched until darkness made it impossible to continue. With a heavy heart, she called a halt for the night.

Wally took care of the horses while she got a fire going. Soon the tangy smell of brewing coffee filled the air.

The young man ambled up to the pot and poured himself a cup. "Miss Emma, maybe after we rest a bit we could fashion some sort of torch and look some more."

She considered the idea, then shook her head. "I'd like nothing better, Wally, but the fact is, these banks are steep, and the water is still high. We might walk right by and never see him." She gazed off toward the churning waters, and drew a ragged breath. "We have to wait til first light. Then we'll start again."

Sleep was a long time coming and when it did, distressing dreams kept her from resting.

The next day dawned gray and overcast. *Please…no more rain* she prayed as they continued their search. Thankfully, the rain held off and the sun soon blazed hot, drying some of the mud, but remnants of the storm continued to hamper progress.

Uprooted trees, a drowned calf, and someone's milk bucket hung in the dense brush emphasized the power of the raging storm. The thought of Ty being caught up in its torrent turned her insides cold.

She had no idea how far they traveled from where Diablo was found. She just kept walking, one foot in front of the other, digging through brush that tore her fingers and scrapped her skin. Several times, they had to expand the search where the flood waters crested higher, moving out to the abundant underbrush.

By sundown, she was exhausted, covered in mud and loosing hope.

Wally snared a rabbit and cooked it for their supper.

She forced herself to eat, washing it down with strong coffee, knowing she needed the nourishment to continue, but anxiety and fear made each swallow difficult.

The growing sense of loss went beyond tears.

Around noon the next day, she spotted a bit of blue cloth snagged on the limb of a downed tree hanging near the edge of the bank. The same blue as Ty's shirt…and stained with blood. She fell to her knees and clutched it to her heart, alternately thrilled and terrified, unable to stop shaking as she rocked back and forth, holding it against her chest.

Please, God, let him be alive. Let him be alive.

"Miss Emma!" cried Wally from the other side of the creek, "are you all right? Did you hurt yourself?"

It took tremendous effort to stand. "I'm fine. I found a piece of his shirt snagged on a tree limb."

"I ain't seen nothin' over here. Soon as I find a spot to cross over, I'll help you look on your side a ways."

The underbrush was not as thick through this section and they made better time, but found no further trace of Ty.

The surge of hope she experienced on finding that scrap of cloth faded with the setting sun. Pain squeezed her heart and sorrow overwhelmed her.

Oh God! He's gone. I may never find him.

Wally stood uncomfortably by and watched as she shattered into a million pieces, holding the bloodied fabric to her broken heart.

He slipped off into the shadows, leaving her alone as she submitted to the grief. She tried to smother the sobs, but anguish overpowered her.

When there was nothing left, she lay down on the bare ground, curled her knees to her chest and fell into a fitful sleep.

"Miss Emma! Miss Emma! Wake up!"

Wally's frantic voice filtered in through the fog of heartache but she refused to wake, unwilling to face a new day without Ty.

A rough shake of her shoulder gave her no choice.

"You gotta get up, ma'am. I found 'im. I found 'im!"

She jerked upright. "What?"

"I found 'im!" His freckled face was by turns happy and sad. "But we gotta hurry. He's hurt real bad, but he's alive! Just like you said, Miss Emma! He's alive!"

She jumped up and grabbed him by the shoulders. "He's alive?"

"Yes, ma'am." His Adams' apple bobbed wildly up and down as he talked. "Not too far from here." He stepped away from her and grabbed a burning log from the fire. "We gotta hurry, though. Not much light." Wally took off downstream and left her to follow.

He led the way around dense brush, fallen trees and rotten logs to a spot where the steep banks of the creek smoothed out to level ground.

"Somehow he made it out and up to a log over there. I almost missed 'im."

She rushed past him and dropped to her knees, tears of joy streaming down her face when she saw him lying face down behind the trunk of a fallen tree, one arm wrapped around a gnarled branch.

"Ty! Ty!" She gently shook him but he didn't respond.

"He's out cold, ma'am. I tried and tried to wake him but he won't."

"Help me roll him over."

They got him on his back and she stifled a gasp. Dried blood covered his face and a deep cut slashed across his forehead. His shirt and pants were torn, bloody and caked with mud. A quick inspection confirmed her fears. "Looks like two bullet wounds. One in his shoulder and one in his thigh. I can't tell if it's still there or went through." She sat back on her heels and looked at Wally. "I think the mud is helping staunch the flow of blood so I'm not going to mess with it right now. Fever's already started. We need to get him home."

"You stay here, ma'am. I'll rig up a travois."

The bulky contraption Indians used to convey people and supplies through the dense undergrowth was difficult for them to manage, so Wally left to get one of the horses. An hour later, they had him back at their camp.

But he didn't wake up.

She heated some water and bathed the gash on his fore-head, thankful it appeared to be nothing more than a graze, refusing to acknowledge how easily it could've killed him. She opted not to tackle his other wounds at this point for fear of causing the bleeding to start up again.

His skin burned hot all over as the fever continued to rise. She mixed some willow bark tea from Lupe's provisions and hoped to get a spoonful through compressed lips, to no avail. She filled a canteen with the brew and saved it for later.

He'll wake up. He has to.

"We need to head home as soon as possible." Wally's calm voice was the only thing keeping her grounded right now. "Tonight even. I can ride ahead and get a wagon, then head back toward you if you think you can handle him alone."

"We are at least two days out from the ranch at the rate we can travel."

"I know, but I could be there before morning and head back with help. Once we got him in a wagon, we can make better time and be home by tomorrow night."

She considered options and realized there weren't any. "Take Midnight, she's faster. I'll ride your horse. We'll hook the travois up to the other one."

In less than an hour, they were ready to go.

"Keep the creek on your left, ma'am, just like how we got here. Moon will be up in an hour or so. It's waning but will give you some light."

She nodded, unable to speak past the fear choking her.

"Keep your rifle handy, too."

His words hit hard. Whoever did this was still out there.

She nodded again.

"He'll make it, Miss Emma. He made it this far, he'll make it the rest of the way."

"I hope so, Wally. I hope so."

Wally waited until she was mounted before he spurred Midnight toward home.

With one last look at her husband, she urged her horse into a slow walk.

The mournful call of a whippoorwill floated along the evening breeze reminding of something Lupe once said. *"Each time you hear a whippoorwills' call, it means another angel just got their wings."*

Swallowing the sob wedged in her throat, she cast tearful her eyes upward. "Please don't take him from me, Lord. Please. Don't take him from me."

CHAPTER
Twenty-Five

SOMETIME BEFORE DAWN, TY MOANED, AND TOSSED around on the makeshift bed.

She stopped, took the canteen of willow bark tea and managed to get him to swallow some before he drifted off again. She knelt beside him, bathing his face with a piece of her shirt. "Don't you die on me, Tyler Roundtree. Don't you dare."

Startled by a noise behind her, she jumped and grabbed the rifle. Heart pounding, she stood beside Ty's immobile body and looked around. Shadows danced in the breeze that carried with it the smell of cow manure, sage and pine. The crack of a breaking limb had her spinning left, rifle aimed toward the sound. A single Longhorn, its impressive rack spanning six feet across, wandered out of the brush. He stopped and glanced at her before swishing his tail and ambling off toward the creek.

Weak with relief, she sat down and rested her head on the travois pole. Who did this? And why? *Once you are home, we can figure it out.*

It took monumental effort to drag herself back into the saddle and move forward, the only thing driving her was the need to get him help.

Delirious with fever, Ty moaned off and on throughout the day but did not wake.

Mind numb with fatigue and fear, she stopped several times to bath his face, and force more of the tea down, refusing to think it may already be too late.

By late afternoon, she was all but asleep in the saddle, so exhausted she had difficulty staying seated.

When Henry suddenly appeared beside her, she swallowed hard and bit back the tears.

They were safe.

The next five days were a blur as she tended Ty's wounds, bathed his heated flesh with cool water, and prayed he would survive. She never left their room, using the chamber pot when nature called, depending on Lupe to bring her meals and the hands to do what needed to be done around the ranch.

She dipped the rag, rung it out slightly, and pressed it to his burning skin. "Please wake up, Ty," she whispered, "please."

Henry tapped on the door. "Any change?"

She shrugged. "The fever was worse yesterday and last night. He was out of his head most of the time, calling for you and others." She didn't mention laying on top of him to keep him on the bed or how he cried for people only he could see to watch out or duck or how he cried out for his mother. And begged someone named Jennie to forgive him.

She cried with him, tried to soothe him with soft words and gentle touches. At last, he rested, albeit fitfully. "I'm not sure but I think his fever is going down some now and he swallows the medicine I give him." She shook her head. "But he won't wake up."

"You need to get some rest, Emma. Sarah made me promise I would run you out for a while so you could."

Even before he finished, she shook her head. "No. I want to be here when he wakes up."

"At least go down and get something to eat, and talk to Rafe. He's worried sick about you both."

Mention of her father made her flinch. She had not thought of him once during this ordeal and conceded he would be worried. "Of course."

She swayed when she stood and Henry steadied her. "You're dead on your feet, Emma. You need to rest."

She dropped the rag in the bowl and headed for the door. "I'll be back in a few minutes."

Ty struggled against the darkness encasing him, willing the pain to stop. He wanted to know the owner of the soft voice invading his dreams, but every time he tried to wake, the blackness pulled him back. He made progress, though, able to hold off the gloom longer each time.

Something sliced its way through the haze of pain and

shadows. Voices? Henry maybe? Or the woman. Images tossed around by his addled mind were nothing more than bits and pieces that overlapped and blended together, their edges jagged and uneven, like some kind of weird patchwork quilt, and made no sense at all. He pushed against the misery, fighting to rouse himself.

His eyelids weighed a ton, and it took tremendous effort to lift them even a slit. Sunlight streamed in through a window to his right. He slowly turned his head toward it, groaning when the movement caused the pain in his head to intensify. *Sonofabitch!*

"Well, there you are. About damn time."

He struggled to open his eyes, grimacing at the scratchiness, he blinked several times and tried to bring his friend in focus. He gave up and closed his eyes. "What happened?"

Henry moved the chair closer to the bed and sat. "Doc got the bullets out but infection had already set in." He ducked his head and blew out a long breath. "If they hadn't found you when they did, you would've died."

Ty tried to concentrate on what he said but the effort made his head pound. "I was shot?"

"You don't remember?"

"No." He took a ragged breath. "How long I been out?"

"Off and on for eight days."

His eyes jerked open, then squinted at the bright light. "Eight days?"

Henry nodded, reached for the brown bottle on the table and poured a small amount of liquid in a spoon. "I'm under orders to make sure you get this. Supposed to help with the pain and the fever. I'm just glad you're awake to take it. It's a bitch trying to get you to swallow when you were out of your head most of the time."

"Water first. I'd probably choke on it right now."

Henry helped him drink and gave him the medication.

Each beat of his heart felt like a bomb exploding in his head. If that sour tasting shit would help, he'd drink a gallon.

He lay back down, eyes closed. "Tell me."

Henry quickly relayed the events of the last week. "She wasn't happy when I said we didn't find you and took off to look herself."

His brow furrowed as he tried to absorb what Henry said. "Sarah did that?" He couldn't imagine why Henry would let his pregnant wife take off looking for him.

"No, not Sarah, Emma."

"W—"

"Oh thank God! You're awake at last!"

Ty squinted at the vision in blue as she hurried forward and placed the food tray she carried on a dresser.

She hastened over and sat on the edge of the bed, pulling his hand in hers. Her smile was radiant. Something about it…

"I was so worried." She clasped his hand gently, rubbing the knuckles with her thumb. "Why didn't you call me? You knew I wanted to be here when he woke up." She directed the question to Henry but never took her eyes off him.

The throbbing intensified to the point he expected his head would explode at any moment. Breath hissing through clenched teeth, he eased his hand from hers and watched as the smile disappeared, highlighting dark circles of fatigue under bewildered emerald eyes.

"Who are you?" he whispered.

CHAPTER
Twenty-Six

S HE STAMMERED, CONFUSED. "WH-WHAT?"

His voice, thick and unsteady, was no more than a hoarse whisper. "Who are you?"

She looked at Henry whose face clouded with concern.

"Ty," he stammered, "its Emma. Your wife."

His eyes jerked open, then squinted against the brightness before fixing on her. "Wife?"

She sat up straight, forced herself to remain calm despite the uncertainty ripping through her. *How can he not remember me?* "Yes."

Henry placed a hand on Emma's shoulder and squeezed. "I'll send one of the boys to town for Doc Morton and the sheriff. He said to let him know as soon as Ty came around."

She clenched her jaw to kill the sob clogging her throat and nodded.

"I'll be right back." He turned and left them alone.

It took monumental effort to speak in a neutral tone. "You seem to remember Henry…what else do you remember?"

He paused. "Not much."

She bit her lip, took a breath. "What exactly is not much?"

Eyes shut, mouth a tight line, he rolled his head slowly side to side, and groaned.

"Are you in pain?"

"Head hurts like a bitch." Without opening his eyes, he continued, "Sorry, ma'am. Didn't mean to cuss."

She fought hard against the tears. Crying wouldn't help anything. "No apology needed." She resisted the urge to add *I'm your wife.*

He didn't remember her. How was that possible?

She reached for the bottle holding Lupe's pain medicine. "This should help."

"Henry gave me some. Any water left?" His voice was gruff and hoarse, his words clipped.

She set it aside and reached for the glass of water on the table. She supported his neck while he drank it all.

With a heavy sigh, his head sank back on the pillow. "We're married?"

"Yes."

"How long?"

She hesitated. "Less than two weeks."

He opened his eyes and blinked several times. "That's all?"

She nodded, smoothed down the front of her skirt. "We married right before you left for the drive." Her face heated with the memory of their lovemaking. *How could he not remember?*

The silence drug on and she thought he drifted off again.

"You came after me."

"Yes."

"Why?" His speech became slurred, and his eyelids fluttered.

"You're my husband."

His eyes slid shut, his chest rose and fell in even movements.

"And I love you," she whispered.

Emma stood at the foot of the bed and watched as Doc Morton examined the patient.

"All things considered, Tyler, I'd say you're doing good."

"How bad?"

"You're a lucky man." He pointed to the gash across Ty's forehead. "A slight turn of your head and we wouldn't be having this conversation. Took a bullet out of your shoulder and you left leg. Nothing vital hit but you lost a lot of blood." He turned to Emma. "Stick to soup and light stuff a few days as he can tolerate it, but take it easy. He's been out of it for a week." He snapped his bag shut. "Keep him still for another week, then try to get him moving around."

"How long before this headache and dizziness goes away?" Ty glanced at Emma, "and why can I remember Henry but not...that I'm married?"

Doc shook his head. "Not surprised you got memory issues. Something put an egg-sized knot on your head."

"How long before it comes back?"

"Can't rightly say. The brain is pretty hardy but yours took a beatin'. We just need to be patient and let it heal." He spoke to Emma. "Lupe's pain concoction will work for his fever, too, if it comes back." He handed her a small brown bottle. "If the pain gets too bad, give him three or four drops of this in a spoon of water. It tastes like…well, it's bad. It'll put him to sleep which is probably best. I'll be back in a few days."

He turned for the door and greeted a newcomer. "Howdy, Sheriff."

"Doc." Sheriff Dawson tipped his hat as he entered the room. "Can I talk to him?"

"All yours."

Tall and rawboned, with snow white hair, Jeff Dawson, sheriff for over a decade, was known for being an honest and fair man who stood toe-to-toe with the rowdiest of cowhands.

He smiled at Emma, his brown eyes kind and gentle. "I stopped in to see Rafe. He seems to be doing some better these days."

"Yes, he does."

He turned to Ty, his voice switching to business. "Wanna tell me what happened to you?"

"Wish like hell I knew."

He glanced at Emma who shrugged slightly. "He can't remember anything about it."

Dawson's brow crinkled and he looked back to Ty. "Nothing?"

"Last thing I remember was sitting on Henry's porch with a cigar."

"When was that?"

"I don't know." His curt reply held a heavy dose of frustration.

"He's been here almost six weeks, Sheriff." She kept her voice devoid of emotion, revealing nothing of her inner turmoil.

"All right, what about enemies? Anyone you know of who might want to harm you?"

Emma gasped and two sets of eyes focused on her.

Sheriff Dawson spoke first. "Something wrong, Miss Emma?"

Too startled to reply right away, a cold knot of fear grew in her stomach. "Walker. He threatened Ty."

"Who's Walker?"

"Why would Walker threaten him?"

The questions came on top of each other and added to her state of anxiety. "He…wasn't happy about our marriage. He told me Ty was good as dead."

She glanced at Ty, whose face darkened with an unreadable emotion.

"Well, I must say I was surprised myself when I got the wedding invite. I thought you and Walker were — "

"I was never, ever going to marry him." Heat raced to her cheeks as her temper flared.

Dawson looked at her a moment, took a breath, and returned to questioning the patient. "Anyone else in your past I need to know about?"

"No. At least not that I can remember. Ask Henry. We've known each other for many years."

"Okay. You remember anything else, get word to me." He turned back to Emma. "I'll talk with Walker but I gotta say, that don't sound like him."

You don't know him like I do.

After he left, Emma busied herself straightening up the

bedroom while avoiding looking at Ty.

"Can we talk?"

She nodded, too distressed to answer his soft-spoken question.

He tried to scoot himself up in the bed but quickly fell back.

"Here, let me help." She maneuvered the pillows behind him, and soon had him sitting upright. She forced herself to ignore the memories swamping her at the proximity of his mouth to hers; the taste of him, the smell of him threatening to dissolve her determination.

He leaned back and puffed out a breath. "Thanks. Hate like hell to be so weak." This time he didn't apologize for cussing but he did look away, the hint of a flush on his bearded cheeks.

She pulled the chair closer to the bed and sat, suddenly so nervous she trembled. *What did he want to talk about? Did he remember something?*

He closed his eyes and she waited for him to speak.

"Were you…involved with him? Walker?"

"Hell no!" She sputtered, bristling with indignation.

His eyes widened, then a ghost of smile tugged up one corner of his mouth. "You cussed."

She met his steady gaze. "Yes, well, I do sometimes. You never minded."

He studied her for several heartbeats before continuing. "Why would he threaten me, then?"

She couldn't sit still so she walked to the window and back before speaking. "Our marriage is …not like most."

"Meaning?"

She took a deep breath and told him.

"So, you're saying because of your father's will, he would use you to get the ranch and tried to scare off anyone who came to call?"

"Yes."

"And you didn't want to marry him?"

"Not if he was the last man on earth."

"But you would marry a total stranger? Someone you know nothing about?"

She chewed on her lip, shy about revealing her love for him but knowing she should. "I knew all I needed to."

His brow creased, and his eyes narrowed. "Which was?"

She returned to the chair, hands folded in her lap. "You're a good man. You respect me." She met his steady gaze. "I trust you. And…I love you."

His jaw clenched, and he remained silent.

"You told me up front you weren't sure you even knew what love was but that you cared for me."

"I did?"

"Yes."

"What else?"

"Well, we talked… about things." Heat rushed to her cheeks and she looked away.

"Like what?"

"Oh, hell!" She moved to the end of the bed and crossed her arms over her chest.

When she looked at him, a ghost of a smile appeared for a heartbeat, then dissolved.

"You didn't mind that I'm not what one would normally expect in wife."

"Why not?"

Her hands fisted on her hips and she blew out a breath.

"Because I'm not very…ladylike. I cuss, I wear britches and work alongside the men, and…"

He stared, eyes narrowed. "And…"

"I can't cook." She folded her arms across her chest again, glanced at him, then quickly away. "And I'd never been kissed…till you showed me how."

CHAPTER
Twenty-Seven

Each tormenting beat of Ty's heart struck his head like a sledge hammer. He closed his eyes against the pain and tried to concentrate on something else. Like the stunningly beautiful Emma, his supposed wife, whom he taught how to kiss. *What else did I teach you?*

He took a steadying breath but couldn't stifle the groan any movement caused. An unexpected wave of nausea added to his distress.

She immediately sat beside him on the bed. "Do you need the pain drops Doc left?"

"No. Just give me a minute."

She sat and waited.

Even in his debilitated state, he recognized the embarrassment she tried to hide as she recalled their relationship. Her answers were straightforward and sincere and she didn't hesitate when he appeared to be in pain.

Is it possible she does love me? Do I…did I love her?

He opened his eyes and found her worriedly searching his face, the fatigue and concern more evident viewed this close. *Because of me.*

"I'm sorry."

She blinked twice. "For what?"

"…Not remembering."

She gave a one-shoulder shrug and looked away, but not before he saw the look of sadness pass over her features. "Not your fault."

His head pounded, but he needed answers. "Maybe if you told me more about us, it would help me remember."

She ducked her head and looked at him from the corner of her eye, chewing on her lower lip, a look so seductive it made his breath hitch and the pounding in his head kick up a notch.

He had an instant of…something…that vanished before he could put a name to it. A momentary flash, a memory perhaps? Had he seen her do that before?

The struggle to latch on to it compounded his headache to the point he feared he might lose the only thing on his stomach…the water and medicine he recently downed. He clamped his jaw shut, willing the nausea to go away, dismayed when it became evident it was too little, too late.

He rolled over and tossed the meager contents of his belly. Right into her lap.

She leaned forward and cradled his head, her voice compassionate and calm. "This too shall pass."

He had no time to consider her composed reaction. His stomach convulsed again and again, the pain in his head so extreme he trembled like a frightened child. No wound he had ever suffered – that he could remember – compared.

The spasms finally subsided and she gently placed his head on the pillow. He heard the swish of material as she moved away. Too miserable to contemplate her actions, he assumed she wanted to get as far away from him as possible. He didn't blame her.

He gritted his teeth as another wave of nausea loomed.

And then she returned, a cool rag brushing over his face, across his mouth, down his neck, each stroke soft and soothing. A delicate, flowery scent teased his nose.

"When you're ready, we'll try some water to rinse your mouth."

He didn't trust himself to speak and movement caused pain so he grunted and hoped she understood.

Apparently, she did because a moment later her hand slid behind his neck and gently lifted. "Just enough to rinse your mouth."

The goblet touched his lips and he obeyed her instructions, swishing the cool liquid around in his mouth, then wondering what to do with it. *Please don't tell me to swallow this nasty tasting crap.*

"Spit it back in the glass."

He tried to, but mostly it dribbled down his chin and onto his chest. He didn't care.

It shamed him to no end to disgrace himself in such a manner and she had to clean him up. If it bothered her at all, he couldn't tell.

A moment later, her hand slid under his neck again. "The pain is obviously worse than you let on so you *will* take the pain drops Doc left. He said it tastes awful but will help you sleep and that's the best thing for you right now."

She leaned forward to help him and another wave of queasiness hit, but, thankfully, passed without incident.

"If it doesn't stay down, we'll just do it till it does."

He dutifully opened his mouth and swallowed, praying the nasty shit would stay down the first time. She eased his head back on the pillow and he took a slow, deep breath willing his body to relax and the trembles to cease. He moaned when the cool rag touched his face again, amazed something so simple could be so comforting. He wanted to apologize for being helpless, for ruining her dress, but the words wouldn't form, and his eyes refused to open so he slowly surrendered to the darkness enveloping him.

He dreamed his fingers threaded through strands of burnished silk soft as a cottony cloud. Something about it soothed him, kept the disjointed, lightning fast images that floated through his head from bringing back the pain. As long as he focused on the silk, the pain abated.

From a distance, a light sound intruded, causing the fantasy to drift away. *No. The pain will come back.*

He fought to keep it, but the dream slowly faded as he came awake and cautiously opened his eyes. A dull ache replaced the incessant throbbing but his mouth and lips were parched as the West Texas desert. He tried to moisten his lips with his tongue but he couldn't produce any spit.

A soft snore drew his gaze to the side. The lamp burned low on the bedside table. She sat slumped over in the chair, upper body lying on the bed, his fingers entwined in the glossy curls laying over her shoulder.

How can anything feel this soft? He ran his fingers through her hair, suffered another of those miniscule, painful flashes, but this time, it was less than when he tried to remember. *Because the silk takes away the pain.*

She moved, and since his fingers were tangled in her hair, it pulled, startling her awake.

He didn't have time to pretend sleep.

Voice groggy, she looked up. "Are you okay?"

"Thirsshty." The lack of moisture made speaking difficult and even to him, his voice sounded gruff and slurred.

She disentangled his hand, turned up the lamp and filled a glass with water.

"It's clean," she said as she slipped her hand under his neck. "In case you are wondering." She raised his head and tipped the glass. "Drink slowly. One sip at a time and swish it around your mouth before you swallow."

He did as she asked and sluggishly downed the contents, heaving a sigh of relief when it didn't immediately return. "Thank you."

"You're welcome."

He paused. "Sorry I woke you."

She responded with a simple wave of her hand and a yawn.

He closed his eyes a moment to regain focus, then looked at her. "This isn't the first time you slept in a chair." The statement came out very matter-of-fact because he intuitively knew the answer.

"I wanted to be here in case you needed anything." Her pale face, haggard with fatigue, nonetheless held strength of spirit and determination.

"You're tired. Even I can see that."

"I'm all right. How's your pain? Do you need anything?"

He suddenly noted the difference in clothing, causing his

cheeks to burn. "I ruined your dress."

A tiny smiled softened her features. "It isn't ruined, Ty. A little soap and water and its good as new."

He liked the sound of his name on her lips. Soft and sweet, her voice flowed through his broken body like Doc's healing tonic. Then another realization hit him. "This is your bedroom."

"It's – was – ours." She looked down then up at him. "I know you don't remember, but I do."

She chewed her lower lip, and he found himself focusing on it. *I taught her to kiss.*

She clasped her hands in her lap. "Doc said it will take some time. We just have to be patient."

She didn't sound patient. She sounded exhausted. "I'm weak as a kitten. Help me move over."

"Why?"

"You need some rest and you can't get it sleeping in that chair."

"I might hurt you."

He hoped his attempt at a smile didn't look like a grimace. "Em, a fly could hurt me right now."

She gasped. "Y-you called me Em."

"I'm sorry…does that bother you?"

The look of hope on her face hit him hard in the gut. Suddenly, he *wanted* to remember, *wanted* to be the man she loved.

"N-no. You call me that sometimes."

"It wasn't a conscious thing…calling you Em, I mean. It just happened."

"I-I know. I'm not – I know."

"Help me scoot over." He pulled the covers back and saw

he had nothing on underneath. He jerked them up again, face so hot, he thought his fever returned. "I'm sorry...I didn't realize..."

She smiled and his heart thumped wildly, and the pain in his head kicked up a notch.

"We're married, Ty." She glanced at his waist, "I've seen it before." She looked longingly at the bed, then back at him. "Are you sure I won't bother you?"

"I'm sure. It's my left side that's hurt, you'll be on the right."

The simple task of scooting across the bed drained him of all energy and his head pounded. "Damn."

She immediately checked his wounds. "Did something happen? Did I hurt you?"

"I'm fine. Just weak. Head hurts like a bitch." He didn't open his eyes as he murmured. "Sorry. I cussed again."

"Well, hell."

He heard the smile in her voice.

"No damn cussing allowed."

Eyes closed against the pain, he attempted a grin. "Lay down, Em."

"Fine, but first you need to take your pain medicine." She reached for the bottle and spoon.

"No. If I get still it will ease up and I can go back to sleep. I don't like how the medicine makes me feel."

She covered her mouth as she yawned. "Okay. I'm too tired to argue." She stood and headed toward the dressing screen in the corner and paused. "It will be dawn soon, no point in getting undressed now." She turned down the lamp, sat on the edge of the bed and removed her shoes. "I'll just rest for a bit."

She lay with her back to him. "I'll give you a shave tomorrow. I'm not liking this whole bearded look." She yawned twice and quickly fell asleep, unaware of the calloused fingers entwined in the healing silk of her hair.

CHAPTER
Twenty-Eight

EMMA WOKE TO SUNLIGHT STREAMING THROUGH HER bedroom window and the warmth of Ty's chest against her cheek, dismayed to note she had drooled on him. She ran her fingers through the springy curls, absently wondering why his chest hair fascinated her so.

Reality swamped her and she stiffened. *What I am doing?* It took several moments for her to come fully awake and remember how she ended up here.

She eased away from him and saw he slept soundly, one hand fisted in her hair. As slowly as possible, she loosened his fingers and stood.

Immediately, Ty groaned and reached out, mumbling in his sleep. She sat down and took his hand. His head rolled from side to side as he shook off her hand and reached for something only he could see.

She leaned forward, speaking softly, "You're dreaming,

Ty. Shhhh…you're safe now." Her hair fell over her shoulder and landed on his hand. He grabbed it, mumbled something that sounded like *silk* and drifted off again.

She lay still and pondered her next step. For some reason, having his hand in her hair seemed to soothe him. Then she remembered the lock retrieved from his tattered clothing. The strands she gave him their last night together. It rested on top of her dresser. On the other side of the bed.

She worked herself free and grabbed the lock even as Ty started mumbling again. She pressed the hair in his hand and his fingers tightened around it, his breathing calmed and he rested easier.

She rigidly held the tears in check. "Oh Ty, a part of you *does* remember." Leaning forward, she pressed a kiss to his bearded cheek. "Rest easy, my love. I'll be back soon."

As she stood, Lupe entered the room, a food tray in her hands.

"Good morning, Señor*a*. He is resting good, no?" Lupe spoke softly as she placed the tray on the dresser. "You both slept good, I think."

Emma glanced outside, distressed to see the mid-day sun. "Oh my! I needed to get the men started checking for strays today." She hurried toward the dressing screen. "Please tell me you have coffee on there."

"*Si,* I do. And lunch which you will eat before you do anything. And besides, you told Wally yesterday to handle that so you sit and eat."

"I did?" She shook her head. "Oh, right. I remember." She came back to the chair. "I can't believe I slept so long." She looked at Ty, the lock of hair clutched to his chest and once again, fought back tears. "Part of him remembers, Lupe," she whispered, then turned grief stricken eyes to her friend. "Part of him remembers."

Lupe bent and hugged her. "Things will work out, Señor*a*. God has his ways. Now, you must eat something and go speak with your father. He is asking for you. I will stay with Señor Ty."

Lupe placed the tray on the side of the bed and pointed. "Eat. I will be back shortly and you will go see your father."

Half an hour later, Emma entered her father's room and smiled when she saw him sitting in his chair by the window. "How did you get here?"

"José helped me. How's Ty?"

Though his voice sounded stronger, his shoulders slumped forward and his skin held a pasty pallor.

"I think he will be fine. How long have you been up? Do you need to go back to bed?"

He shook his head and continued to look out the window, eyes moving around as he surveyed the yard.

"Need another swing on that old tree there." He nodded toward the tree on the right.

She didn't miss the note of melancholy in his voice.

"You sure loved to swing."

She placed a chair beside him and sat down. "I remember Sarah and me taking turns to see how high we could go." She grinned. "Mama didn't much like us doing that."

He looked at her and a muscle twitched in his jaw. "You're not getting enough rest worrying about me and him, too."

"I'm fine, Papa. In fact, I slept for several hours last night." She adjusted the blanket across his knees. "Ty slept good, too." *Clutching my hair in his hand.*

"His memory coming back at all?"

She lifted one shoulder, and shook her head. "Not really. Doc said it will take some time. But he wants to remember and tries to…but, well, it's still too soon to expect anything."

His gnarled hand covered hers and squeezed. "He'll remember in time. He will."

She didn't reply, merely gave a half-hearted smile.

He ducked his head, then looked at her again. "I know you think I have doubts about you being able to handle this place when I'm gone."

She didn't have the strength to argue with him today. "We can talk about that another time."

"Dammit, girl, listen to me!"

His stern voice caused her to flinch.

"I ain't never for one minute thought you couldn't run this place. Never!"

"But –"

"I wanted to know you'd be happy without me." He took her hand again. "The way you went after Ty…the look on your face. I knew then you loved him. That's all I ever wanted for you, Emma Rose…to find somebody to love like I loved your Ma." He shook his head and his voice trembled. "I know I went about it all wrong, but I ain't got much time. I had to know my baby girl would have someone to love."

Her heart seized at the love on his face.

"And she does."

Tears clogged her throat. "He doesn't remember me, Papa." Her voice cracked. "He doesn't remember."

And then he did the one thing she had no defenses against.

He pulled her to him in a clumsy embrace.

She couldn't remember the last time he hugged her. That

realization shattered the last vestige of control and she made no effort to stop the hot tears rolling down her cheeks.

Rafe tightened his embrace and she sobbed harder.

A rustle of movement penetrated the veil of sleep and Ty focused on the sound, anticipating the headache that accompanied waking. Satisfied he would only be subjected to a dull throb for the moment, he gradually opened his eyes.

His *wife* stood with her back to him, messing with something on the dresser…wearing pants. Tight pants. He blinked several times as his eyes focused on the well-formed derriere that twitched as she moved.

"I let you wear pants?" His croaky voice held a note of disbelief.

She squeaked and spun around. Surprise quickly became pissed off.

"Let me?" Her hands fisted on her hips and her chin came up. "You *let* me wear pants?"

Rendered speechless by the passion in her eyes, the play of light on her hair which draped her shoulders like a tobacco-colored shawl, he stared.

She stood beside the bed, emerald orbs flashing fire. "Now see here, Tyler Roundtree, that piece of paper is a marriage certificate not a bill of sale!" She puffed out a breath. "I realize you are not yourself right now, but you do not *let* me do anything!"

With sudden clarity, he knew. They had a similar discussion before. And he lost. He chased the elusive memory like a hound after a rabbit, almost had it, then it bounded away, leaving only the damnable headache. He compressed his lips against the groan hung in his throat and closed his eyes.

"Oh, no!"

The bed sagged when she sat down and placed a soft hand on his arm.

"I'm so sorry! I didn't mean to upset you. Do you need the pain drops?"

A grunt had to suffice for a reply as he battled an unsettled stomach, his other constant companion.

She shifted on the bed, one hand resting on his arm. "I have the basin if you're going to be sick again."

He willed himself not to, focusing instead on the warmth of her touch, the gentleness of her voice.

His brain pulsed with flashes that appeared and left before his mind's eye distinguished one from another. Though he couldn't say he actually remembered something, a part of him accepted her as his wife. He cared for her.

The nausea passed a little quicker this time. The pain lessened to a bearable stage. He opened his eyes to find her staring at him, face pinched with concern.

"I'm sorry I upset you."

It took two attempts to speak. "Not you. Memory."

She sat up straighter, eyes bright with anticipation. "You remembered something?"

"Not exactly." He closed his eyes and concentrated on what he wanted to say, ignoring the pain. "It's like a memory is right there. When I try to…to latch on to it, the pain starts and I lose it."

Her hand slid slowly up and down his arm, her touch a soothing balm to his soul.

He sighed and looked at her. "We argued before, didn't

we? About you wearing pants?"

She lowered her eyes, stains of pink high on each cheek. "Well, we didn't exactly argue since you, um, you…"

"I what?"

She avoided making eye contact. "You…liked me in them."

"I did?" *I can sure see why.*

"Uh-huh." She glanced at him and lowered her eyes, golden-brown lashes sweeping down. "You said – " She straightened and met his steady gaze. "Aw hell. You said you should stop me from wearing them before you had to kick someone's ass for looking at mine."

A smile edged up the corner of his mouth. "Did I? Have to kick someone's ass?"

She blew out a breath. "No. But we were only together only a couple of days before you left for the drive."

He snorted, the sound rusty from lack of use. "I bet we argue a lot."

"Why do you say that?"

"We're very different."

"Men and women usually are."

He didn't disagree.

She shifted on the bed and faced him. "We talked about our differences and agreed to accept each other as we are… good, bad, and otherwise."

He couldn't imagine having such a deep discussion with anyone let alone someone he supposedly barely knew. But at the same time, it felt…*right.*

"What else?"

The color on her cheeks heightened but she didn't look away.

"You said the best part of arguing…" Her gaze dropped to his lips. "…was making up afterwards."

The instant flash of desire the remark garnered surprised him. *Well, parts of me obviously remembers something.* "Did we…make up often?"

Her voice dropped to a sexy whisper and desire kicked up a notch. So did the throbbing in his head. He ignored it.

Her gaze held his for several heartbeats. "A couple of times."

He shifted his attention to the vee in her shirt where the top button strained against full breasts. The flicker of yet another not-exactly-a-memory played hide-and-seek with his brain and he had to close his eyes and breathe deeply before speaking. "What's this?" He held up the long strand of hair.

"A piece of my hair."

"Where did I get it?"

She paused. "I gave it to you before you left." The flicker of a smile bloomed then faded. "You like touching my hair." She smoothed out the rumpled bed covers. "I put it in your hand this morning when I had to get up because you grew so restless when I left."

He rubbed the silken curls between his thumb and index fingers. "It's so soft."

The tenderness in her expression left him speechless.

"Lupe made some light soup for you. I know you probably don't feel much like eating but you have to try. I'll help you sit up."

He didn't bother to disguise his lack of enthusiasm for the idea. "It probably won't stay down."

"One way to find out."

Once positioned to her liking, she strode to the dresser

and returned with his dinner

She placed the basin within reach then sat beside him on the bed, bowl and spoon in her hand.

"We'll do this slow and easy. One spoon at a time. If you start feeling ill, tell me right away."

His eyes were drawn to the top button so he shut them and concentrated on not throwing up as she brought the spoon to his lips. The thick soup, warm, lightly spiced and filled with tiny chunks of vegetables, delighted his taste buds, and he prayed he would not need the basin as he swallowed the first spoonful.

It appeared the more he ate, the hungrier he got and in no time at all, the bowl was empty.

"How do you feel?" A faint tremor filtered through her voice as though some strong emotion touched her.

"Like I could eat a gallon of it."

Joy bubbled in her laugher. "I'd say that's a good sign." She placed the empty bowl on the tray and returned it to the dresser. "When you're ready, I'll give you a shave."

He kept his eyes closed, enjoying the moment. "You don't like the beard?"

"Ummm, not really. It makes you look, well, fierce."

Surprised, he opened his eyes. "Fierce?"

The bed sagged when she sat back down. "Like a pirate might look. Did you have a beard before?" Her brow furrowed and her expression grew serious as she studied his face.

"No. Well, during the war, I'd go some time without shaving, but never really liked a beard."

"Is that how you got the scar? In the war?"

He scowled and rubbed the white streak on his jaw. "Yes."

"I'm sorry. I didn't mean to bring up bad memories."

"I didn't tell you before?"

She shook her head. "We never talked about it."

"Were we happy?" His question made her flinch and he wondered if he really wanted to know the answer.

She rubbed her palms on jean-clad thighs, then straightened her shoulders and faced him. "The first few days were…a challenge, but after we…after…" The pink on her cheeks turned bright red and she turned away.

Suddenly, he knew what *after* meant. "I'm sorry, I didn't – I just…"

She shook her head and kept her back to him. "Like I said before, ours is not a typical marriage. We were married for three days before we – you know, and then you had to leave on the drive." She looked at him and continued. "We had — have — a bond, a friendship, if you will. It's very strong and started before we ever married."

"You said you loved me."

"I do," she whispered.

When she smiled at him, his heart turned over. The transformation left him speechless.

"I know you don't believe it's true, but it is. I fell in love with you the first time I ever saw you though I admit it took some time for me to realize that's what it was. You're a kind and honorable man. You are my husband and I love you." She leaned forward and placed a soft kiss on his bearded cheek. "Nothing will ever change that."

He remained silent as she rose and walked out, afraid words would break the spell she cast over him.

How could I ever be worthy of such love?

CHAPTER
Twenty-Nine

"WHAT ARE YOU DOING?" EMMA THREW THE armful of laundry she carried onto the nearest chair as she hurried to where Ty sat on the edge of the bed.

"Doc said I should try to move around after a week. It's been over a week." He tugged at the sheet resting across his lap. "I'm going nuts lying here with nothing to do but think about the shit I can't remember."

She let out a deep breath. "You've remembered a few things."

"Hell, gathering strays and nearly getting tossed by my horse doesn't count."

"There've been other memories, too. And it's a start. Doc said it would take some time." She watched the color of his eyes change from soft slate to a stormy grey as he spoke.

"I haven't remembered us, Em." His voice shook with

emotion. "What if I don't remember? What then?"

"Don't borrow trouble, Ty." She kept her voice calm and positive, though she felt neither. "It will come in time."

"And if it doesn't?"

"We'll cross that bridge when we come to it." She went to the beautifully carved oak armoire her father had made for her and sifted through his clothing. "Let's see if we can get you dressed."

"How can you be so calm about this?" His voice vibrated with controlled tension.

She sat beside him on the bed, clothing clutched in her hands. "I'm not calm, Ty. I'm scared." She took a deep breath. "But I'm also hopeful these little things you've remembered will slowly lead to bigger things." She lifted something from the pile on her lap. "Maybe getting you up and about where you can look around will help."

"What's that?" He pointed to the black drawers she held.

"I didn't think your jeans would slide on over your leg yet so I made these drawers for you to wear. They're loose-fitting and tie at the waist so it shouldn't bother your leg. And you can wear them around the house till you're ready for jeans again."

"They're black."

"Would you rather I used the pink dress with the yellow flowers on it?"

"You made these?" He looked skeptical.

"Well, Lupe helped me." She shook them out. "Let's see if they fit."

Half an hour later, he sat in a chair by the window in his new drawers and a shirt. Getting his injured arm through the sleeve and back into the sling proved to be the biggest challenge. "Damn. I didn't think I would be this weak."

"You've been through a lot in the last two weeks or so." She stood behind his chair, barely subduing the urge to wrap her arms around him. "Do you want to sit here a while or would you like to try and walk around some?"

"I think I better stick with just sitting here for now." He turned to face her, paused and spoke softly, "Thank you."

She smiled. "You're welcome. Oh, got a telegram from Leo yesterday. They might hit Ft. Worth a few days early. They might even be headed back by the end of next week."

"What about the new Herefords?"

They both started at his question then spoke at once.

"You remembered the Herefords!"

"I remembered something."

This time, she didn't resist and leaned over to wrap her arms around him. "That's wonderful!"

Using his good arm, he took her hand and pulled her around until she stood in front of him. "Your horse threw you," he whispered, "and you fell asleep in front of me on the way home."

She forced a timid smile. "I did."

They stared at each other for several moments before Emma spoke. "I have to go check on Papa and see if there was any significant damage from the storm last night." She kissed his forehead. "I'll see you later. Lupe will be around if you need anything."

Emma glided down the stairs to her father's room, happier than she had been since the day Ty left her under the oak tree. His condition improved more each day and after the night he insisted she lie down beside him, she continued to do so. Granted she was fully clothed but she did not plan for that to continue much longer. She wanted her husband back.

His memory of our time together is returning. Just yesterday he remembered pieces of our first official meeting in my office.

The moment she opened the door to Rafe's room, her good mood vanished.

Hank Walker rose from his chair beside her father as she entered. "Well, if it isn't the lovely Mrs. Roundtree. Always a delight to see you, Em."

"Don't call me that." She didn't bother to disguise her dislike as she moved toward her father. "What's he doing here?"

Before Rafe replied, Walker cut him off. "I have business with your father."

"What business?"

"Nothing you should be concerned about."

"If it concerns my father or this ranch, it concerns me."

"He brought the deed to the Brantley place over."

Rafe's voice held a hint of impatience though she wasn't sure if it was with her or Walker. "Did you change the combination on the safe? He couldn't get it open."

"Yes." *After I found this snake in there acting like lord of the manor.* "I thought you just leant him money for those repairs?"

"Doug Brantley is too proud for his own good," chided Walker, "insisted on giving Rafe the deed until he paid it back." He pulled a folded document from his coat pocket. "Give me the combination, and I'll put this away."

"No need." She held out her hand. "I'll take care of it later."

A dangerous glint flashed in his eyes and quickly disappeared. "Of course." He handed it to her, fingers brushing hers in the process. "Whatever you say, Mrs. Roundtree." His unpleasant smile never reached his eyes. "How is your husband these days?"

Emma forced herself to remain calm, despite the anxiety she felt in his presence. "Better." She turned to her father. "Do you need anything before I go?"

Rafe's troubled look bounced from her to Walker. "I'm good. When will you be back?"

"Couple of hours."

"I'll keep Rafe company for a while. I know he's tired of being by himself all the time."

She refused to rise to the bait. "I want you gone before I get back."

A quick kiss to her father's forehead and she left without a backward glance, refusing to react to the prickle of unease creeping up her spine as she walked out.

CHAPTER
Thirty

TY GRUNTED AS HE HEFTED HIMSELF FROM THE CHAIR and limped toward the bed. *I'd give my eye teeth for a cup of coffee right now.* So much so, he considered the advisability of trying to make it down the stairs without falling, but finally admitted it was foolish to try alone.

"Mind if I come in?"

His gaze jerked to the man in the doorway, annoyed to realize he hadn't heard him approach.

The stranger didn't wait for Ty to answer before he walked in. "Heard about what happened."

About six-feet tall, he wore a dark suit and tie and while something about him rang familiar, he couldn't exactly place him. Instinct, however, had Ty on full alert. Whoever this man was, he didn't like him.

"Glad to see you are up and about."

The concern voiced didn't match the hooded expression

on his face and the hair on the back of Ty's neck bristled. *Evil eyes.* "Thanks."

The man tapped the bowler hat he held lightly against his thigh. "You don't remember me." A tight smile accompanied the succinct statement. "I'm Hank Walker."

Ty's memory returned in fits and starts, usually in fragments and out of the blue. Like now. "The attorney." *And an asshole.*

A worried shadow crossed Walker's face. "I heard you couldn't remember anything."

"What do you want, Walker?"

Recovering, the man smirked. "Word around town is you got shot and nearly died."

"As you can see, I'm still here."

His uninvited guest looked around the room, eyes coming to rest on Emma's chemise which topped a pile of clothing on the back of a chair.

The way Walker eyed her undergarment pissed him off but there wasn't a damn thing he could do about it. Not now, anyway. "What the hell do you want?" He didn't bother to disguise his displeasure as he repeated his question.

"Emma seems to think I had something to do with your accident."

"Did you?"

His jaw clenched and released. "I had nothing to do with what happened to you."

Ty raised one brow but didn't reply.

"She spouted off to the sheriff. He questioned me."

When Ty remained silent, Walker slapped his hat against his leg with a little more force. "I didn't appreciate being questioned. Bad for my business."

"She must have had a good reason." *Where the hell is my gun?*

Walker straightened, superior smile in place. "She got mad because I wouldn't marry her." He positioned the hat on his head. "Women do the craziest things when they're pissed."

It took all Ty's control not to reveal the depth of his rage as he envisioned planting his fist in the middle of his obnoxious face. Several times. "You and I both know that's a lie."

"Are you sure?"

His smirk was more than Ty could handle. His voice cool and controlled, he eyed the attorney. "Remember today, Walker. Remember it when I am come after you."

"Señor Ty – " Lupe stopped in the doorway and glared at the attorney. "What are you doing in here?"

"I was just leaving." He glanced at Ty as he stopped and ran a finger over the edge of the chemise. "She's lovely in this." He tapped the brim of his hat. "I look forward to our next meeting." He nodded to Lupe and sauntered down the stairs whistling softly.

Ty maintained a death grip on the mattress, anger causing his head to pound. *Bastard touched her gown.*

Lupe carefully set the tray on the foot of the bed. "Señor Ty? Are you all right?"

It took two deep breaths before he spoke with any measure of control. "Did she want to marry him?" He ground out the words through clenched teeth.

"No!" Lupe shook her head. "She does not even like him. I think she fears him, but do not know why."

He nodded toward the garment Walker defiled with his touch. "Burn that. Now."

"*Si,* Señor." She grabbed up the gown and turned back to

him. "There is more soup and some coffee."

Ty concentrated on control. The hammering in his head matched the rapid thump of his heart, memories flashing in and out, as nausea returned with a vengeance. He clamped his jaw tight, breathing slowly through his nose, trying to ward off disaster.

"Señor Ty?"

Lupe's concerned question helped him focus and tamp down the queasiness. "I'm fine. Headache's back."

"Maybe the coffee and soup will help."

He doubted he could keep anything down at the moment, but didn't say so. "Yeah, maybe. I'll wait a bit to be sure. I need to lie down."

"I understand." She picked up the tray and sat it on a nearby stool, then moved to help him.

"I can do it, thank you."

She stepped back and waited until he appeared settled. "She loves you, Señor Ty," she declared, then turned and left the room.

CHAPTER
Thirty-One

Walker did something to hurt her. Ty woke from yet another restless nap with that thought still bouncing around his head and made up his mind to find out exactly what as soon as she came home.

Stiff muscles protested as he rolled over and sat on the side of the bed. He barely stifled a sigh of gratitude when he discovered the headache all but gone. He slid his injured arm from the sling and gingerly rotated it around, noting it moved better than yesterday. He glanced at his makeshift clock – the window – and surmised it was close to supper time, then saw the food tray on the stool by the bed.

Food and Emma. Two things guaranteed to restore good humor.

His gaze locked on the tray. Real food this time. And coffee.

He reached for the cup first, happy to discover it was still warm. He inhaled the heady aroma and smiled as he took a tentative sip, wary of how his stomach might react to the strong brew. He exhaled slowly as the tepid liquid slid down his throat, then paused before taking a deep mouthful, letting his tongue bask in the pungent flavor before swallowing. Confident it would stay down, he emptied the cup in three deep gulps, certain he felt it already coursing through his veins, restoring his energy.

His stomach growled in hunger as he eyed the steak, potatoes and green beans on the plate. He idly wondered who he should thank for the gravy covered meat being cut into bite-size pieces – Lupe or Emma.

He pulled the stool close to the bed and ate slowly, pausing between bites, partly to make sure it would stay down but mainly to savor the rich gravy and tender meat. All too soon, he eyed the empty plate and wished for another cup of coffee.

"Well, glad to see your appetite's back." Emma entered with a cup in each hand, jean clad hips swaying as she walked toward him. "I debated about leaving a cup when I brought up the tray. Wasn't sure how long you would sleep but knew you would want another one after you ate."

"Thank you." He grinned and ruefully shook his head. "I think I inhaled the other one."

Amusement flickered in her eyes. "No stomach issues? Headache?"

"None. Thank God."

"Good." She sat down beside him, cup cradled in her hands. "Not much to report about last night."

The next few minutes passed with a discussion of the aftermath of the previous nights' thunderstorm.

He drank his coffee as he listened, enjoying the sound of

her voice, the happiness radiating from it as she talked about the ranch and tried to keep his wandering eyes off the top button of her shirt.

"We can have some pretty intense storms this time of year, but luckily last night wasn't one of them."

He grunted. "I can't believe I slept through it."

"Well, you've been pretty restless the last couple of nights so taking the pain medicine to sleep was a good idea. You need the rest."

"I don't want to take any more if I can help it. It's worse than a hangover. Takes me half a day to get over it."

"Well, if you can't sleep tonight, we'll try something else."

Immediately, his mind drifted to things he knew would guarantee him a peaceful sleep – if it didn't kill him – as his eyes wandered back to the button. Afraid his thoughts would be revealed in his face, he looked away and changed the subject. "Where's my gun? I feel naked without it. And would you send Wally up when he has time? I'd like for him to make me some kind of crutch I can use to walk around." He rubbed his face. "I need a real bath, too. Using the basin and rag ain't cutting it anymore."

Her musical laugh lifted his spirits higher and momentarily overshadowed thoughts of Walker's visit.

"Let's see…your gun is in the top drawer of the dresser." She placed her cup on the tray next to his. "Would you like to try and bathe tonight?"

"What time is it?"

"A little after seven."

He shook his head. "Tomorrow's good. Maybe if Wally could get me that crutch I might be able to make it downstairs to the room where the tub is."

"I'll get word to him to tonight. Where do you want me to put the gun?"

"Just bring it to me, if you don't mind."

She handed him the holstered pistol. "I'm guessing you've been in bed all day. Would you like to sit a while?"

He hung the weapon over the bedpost. "I managed to hobble to the chair a time or two today but mostly just lay here, so yeah, the chair."

Once situated, she faced him with hands on her hips, a big smile on her face. "You look more like your old self every day."

"I got a look at myself in your mirror today, so I'm not so sure that's a good thing."

Her smile faltered, returned. "It is to me."

"Why are you afraid of Walker?" The words were out before he could stop them.

Her head snapped back and the bright smile disappeared.

"He came by today. I know something happened."

Fear, stark and real glittered in her eyes, and she gasped, "Here? He came to see you?"

He reached for her hand, careful not to hold too tight. "Tell me what happened, Em."

She licked her lips and rubbed her free hand on her hip, tension radiating from her in rapid pulses. "N-nothing – I – he ..."

Another flash of memory invaded but he held on to it this time. "No lies, between us, Em. We promised...no lies."

She stared as comprehension dawned. "You remembered." Her shoulders sagged and she blew out a long breath. "Let me sit down."

She pulled a chair beside his then moved it where she

faced him and sat, their knees touching. Hands clasped in front, she studied him a moment. "What did he say?"

He didn't understand her reluctance, but intuitively knew they had this conversation before. "Among other things, he said you had the sheriff question him about my accident."

"I did."

"Why?"

She looked down at her hands, then back to him. "Remember when Sheriff Dawson came to see you?"

He nodded, since he vaguely recalled the conversation, though at the time, he still wasn't thinking clearly.

"I told him then he threatened you. Well, he sort of threatened you. After we married."

"Is that the only reason you're afraid of him? Because you believe he threatened me?"

The silence lingered and he thought she might not answer.

"No." Her voice dropped to a soft whisper. "It's not."

His injured arm protested as he reached for her hands, surprised to feel how cold they were. "Tell me."

Mossy green eyes, filled with apprehension, searched his.

Unsure of what she needed from him in order to continue, he simply rubbed his thumbs across her knuckles and waited.

"You asked me before and I couldn't answer."

His body tensed, visions of all the things that *might have* happened turned his blood cold. He cleared his throat – twice – before he spoke. "I have to know, Em. I need the truth because my imagination is making me crazy."

The tensing of her jaw betrayed the level of anxiety she suffered. "He didn't…physically hurt me, Ty. It was – just something he said. If I tell you, it will make you angry."

"Dammit, Em! I'm already angry. In fact I'm mad as hell." Visions of him touching her clothes turned his voice hard as stone. "Tell me. Now."

She rolled her hands over and gripped his tightly. She sat up straight and met his gaze without flinching. "They were just words, Ty. Words I shouldn't let bother me, but they do."

"He threatened you, didn't he?" He struggled with the powerful urge to go after Walker. *Like I can do anything now if I caught the bastard.* "Didn't he?"

"…In a manner of speaking. He's a snake. I don't like him or trust him. And neither do you." She paused. "The exact words don't matter, but when you are ready, I *will* tell you, because I know you will go after him." The hint of a smile emerged as she continued with quiet resolve. "And I will happily stand by and watch you stomp the sorry bastard's ass into the dirt."

Accustomed to hearing her swear on occasion, her statement nonetheless, caught him off guard. He blinked twice, then burst out laughing. A deep, rich, full-hearted laugh. *It feels so damn good to laugh again!*

She tried and failed to stifle her own giggles which soon deteriorated into undiluted laughter.

"You are a pistol, Red." He wiped tears from his eyes as he laughed. "I never know what – " He stopped when he realized she no longer laughed with him. "What is it? What's wrong?"

"You called me Red."

CHAPTER
Thirty-Two

Emma's heart pounded so hard she could hardly breathe. She watched the play of emotions across Ty's face as he concentrated, and pinpointed the exact moment the memory surfaced.

"Red," he repeated softly.

A choked sob escaped as Ty pulled her onto his lap.

"My beautiful Red."

She cupped his face in her hands. "You're back." She kissed him, lightly, tenderly, a kiss for her tired soul to melt into.

Strong hands circled her waist, and pulled her to him as he smothered her lips with a commanding kiss.

She trembled at the urgency of it, feeling the loss when he pulled back a few inches.

He pillowed his head on her chest, arms tightening around her, the warmth of his breath seeping through her shirt.

After a bit, he pulled away and leaned back in the chair.

His brows pulled together when he spoke. "The damn gaps are still there." The line of his mouth tightened, then relaxed. "I remembered seeing you walk into the parlor on our wedding day."

Her body shivered when his expression changed from confusion to desire.

"You took my breath away." He pulled her hands to his lips and pressed kisses across her knuckles. "And I remember that night by the creek, but not much about getting shot." He blew out a breath. "It's the damnedest thing how stuff comes back. All bits and pieces in no particular order."

His slow, sexy smile caused heat to pool in her middle.

"Which probably explains why I had so much trouble sleeping lately."

She cocked her head to one side. "I don't understand."

"Having you beside me at night, wanting to pull you in my arms…" His voice trailed off.

"Why didn't you?"

"There's so much I don't remember…I didn't think I… had the right."

She nibbled her bottom lip. "I wanted so much to touch you, to kiss you." She lowered her lashes, then peeked up at him. "I kept remembering something you told me."

"What?"

"You said I should touch you, kiss you anytime I wanted to." She ducked her head again as her cheeks burned. "But you didn't remember…" Her whispered statement failed to hide the pain it generated.

He pulled her to him. "I'm so sorry for the hell I've put you through." He kissed her softly. "I don't deserve you." This time, his kiss held a dreamy intimacy that foretold of things to come. With a soft groan, he shifted in the chair and pulled back.

"Oh no! I'm hurting your leg."

He stopped her when she made a move to get up. "Red, my leg is not the problem right now."

Heat flooded her face when the *problem* moved against her hip. "We can't…not now!"

He palmed her breast, his thumb rubbing the hardened tip. "Why not?"

"You're hurt."

"Not that hurt." His mouth replaced his hand as he nibbled her through the fabric, fingers working the buttons lose. "Now I know why this damn button fascinated me so." He pushed her shirt open. "Some part of me remembered what was inside."

Her breath caught as he nipped at her breast.

The soft click of the door closing made her jump. "Oh no! Lupe must have seen us!"

He ate away at her composure. "Does she know we're married?"

"Of c-course."

His mouth continued its assault on her concentration.

"Did she shut the door?"

"…Y-yes." Her hands gripped his shoulders as she leaned back to allow him more access.

"I need you, Red." His nostrils flared as he sucked in air, eyes turning the color of storm clouds flashing with silver lightening. He placed her on her feet, then pushed himself from the chair. He ran his hands down her hips, pulling her to him. "I don't deserve you, but God I need you."

She had a moment – a heartbeat – of hesitation before

she sat on the edge of the bed and pulled off her boots.

Ty woke to the warmth of his wife cuddled up beside him, her hair tumbled across his chest, her breath teasing his nipple with each exhale as her fingers played with the hair on his chest. His bruised and battered body ached like the devil but his soul knew peace for the first time in…forever.

Memories flashed like points of light through his mind, some clear, some vague. Emma riding hell bent for leather as they raced for the house, her laughter floating on the air around him, filling his heart with joy; eating supper together as they discussed ranch business. And teaching her to kiss. To make love.

His heart thumped wildly as each new recollection surfaced. He was back.

At last.

Emotion clogged his throat and he pulled her tighter against him, inhaling the fragrance uniquely Emma.

His wife.

"Mmmm," She slid her leg over his, fingernails raking across his chest.

Renewed desire hit him like a gut punch. His injured arm protested when he pulled her on top of him and he barely noticed the pain when her leg grazed his wounded thigh.

She gathered her hair and pulled it over one shoulder, her provocative eyes playful, one corner of her mouth tilted up in smug smile. "Again?"

He slid calloused hands over her creamy flesh, and cupped her bottom, pressing down. "What do you think?"

She leaned in and kissed him. A slow, sensual kiss that nearly sent him over the edge.

"I taught you that?" He flinched when he realized his thought was spoken out loud.

"Uh-huh," she nipped at his lower lip, "I learn quick." She gifted him with a seductive smile. "You taught me other stuff, too."

Momentarily speechless, he uttered softly, "I did?"

She eased down his body. "Shall I demonstrate?"

"I'd die a happy man."

He didn't die; but he did sleep – eventually.

CHAPTER
Thirty-Three

Emma stood beside the bed and watched Ty sleep, savoring the sense of satisfaction engulfing her. Her life was whole again, complete. She would die before she allowed anything to come between them again. One knee on the bed, she leaned over and kissed him awake.

Ty groaned and pulled her to him.

She slipped out of his grasp and stood there, hands on her hips, wearing his discarded shirt, and a smile. "Time to wake up sleepy head."

His hot gaze slid over her body, sending flames to her core.

"Damn. My shirt looks a helleva lot better on you than it ever did on me."

Gooseflesh joined with the heat coursing through her. "Think so?"

"Know so." He sat up in the bed, lips curing upward in a

wickedly sensual smile. "Come here."

She laughed and stepped back. "I have work to do." She sifted through the clothes on the chair. "I know I brought my chemise in yesterday."

"I told Lupe to burn it."

The sudden change in his voice from sinfully seductive to barely controlled anger made her spin around. "Why did —" The drastic change in him from a moment ago stole her voice.

Face blotched purple, he clutched the sheet in his good hand, and a dark vein pulsed in his temple. Lips tightly compressed, he barely got the words out. "Walker touched it."

Her heart slammed. "He what? When?" She dropped the pants she held on the floor and backed away as though it were a snake.

"Yesterday. When he came in here. I told Lupe to burn it."

"Did he touch anything else?" She quivered in indignation, and her voice broke. "Did he?"

"No, he didn't." His voice softened with concern. "Come here."

"He touched my things," she whispered.

"Dammit, Em, come here."

She backed away until her backside hit the bedpost, then turned panicked to eyes to Ty. "I'll burn it all. Anything he touched."

He inched forward, reached for her hand, and pulled her to him. "Emma…he didn't touch anything else, just the chemise and Lupe took it away."

He cupped her chin and made her face him. "I swear to you, Em…that was all."

She released a heavy sigh. "What did he want with you? I left him with Papa."

"I don't know. Seemed pretty surprised when I remembered him."

He rubbed his thumb over her lower lip. "What did he say, Em? Why does he frighten you so?"

She turned worried eyes to him, took a deep breath, and told him about the incident on the porch the night they got married; how Walker's words intimidated and frightened her.

"It's just words, I know it. He's never really *done* anything, but," she shook her head and looked at him. "I'm not a coward, I can face just about anything." She looked down at their clasped hands. "I don't know what it is about him that bothers me but something does. I tell myself he was bluffing, trying to frighten me and I shouldn't let it bother me but it did. You have to promise me you won't do anything about it. Not yet."

She heard his teeth snap together when his jaw clamped tightly shut, saw the anger etched in the tight lines on his face. She grabbed the hand fisted in his lap. "Promise me, Ty."

He turned to face her. "I promise you this, Em…that bastard will never hurt you. Ever." He straightened, rolled his hurt arm around. "And under no circumstances are you to be alone with him ever again."

She opened her mouth to protest his *order*, then quickly shut it when she noted his fierce scowl. "Okay."

The taunt lines in his face softened, and the ghost of a smile appeared. "I'm willing to bet that's a first."

"What is?" She strived to maintain an air of innocence.

A raised brow sufficed for his answer.

"Okay. It is. But don't think I will always be so agreeable."

He pulled her onto his lap, hands circling her waist. "I'm counting on it."

"Why?"

He nibbled her earlobe. "So we can make up afterwards."

Her head lolled to the side as his lips moved down her neck to the base of her throat then back to her lips.

Hungry, demanding, his kiss sent shivers of desire through her.

With great effort, she pushed back. "I have to get going. I have a lot to do today."

She moaned softly as his hand slid over her thigh, under the shirt to cup her breast.

"Sure you can't stay and play?"

She squirmed as he tweaked the hardened tip with his fingers, then covered it with his mouth, dampening the fabric.

"Ohhhh…Ty…"

He took her with him as he fell back on the bed, pulling the shirt over her head with his good arm.

Intoxicated by the rasp of his chest against her nipples, she moved sluggishly back and forth before taking him into her body, yielding to a burning need she knew only he could fulfil.

They abandoned themselves to the molten passion they shared, riding the crest together, before collapsing in a heap on the other side.

She buried her face in the corded muscles of his chest, felt his uneven breathing on her head as they struggled to regain control.

"You're killing me, Red." His voice held a hint of satisfied amusement.

"At least you can stay in bed all day." She pushed herself

up and looked at him. "I have work to do."

He grunted as he pushed the hair from her face and gathered it with his good hand. "I don't plan on staying in bed all day. It's time I got up and moved around."

"You really think you should?"

His smile made her insides flutter.

"If I can do *this* and not pass out, I think I can manage to walk around the house." He lifted one shoulder. "Besides, I'd like to talk to Rafe, let him see I'm doing good."

Warmth spread through her and she nodded. "He'd like that. He asks about you all the time."

"All the more reason for me to see him today."

She rolled to the side of the bed and walked to the armoire, unashamed of her nakedness in front of him. "Need some help getting dressed?"

He snorted. "Not if you want to get out of here anytime soon."

She walked back to him and cupped his face. "I love you, Tyler Roundtree."

He grabbed her hand as she turned away. "I told you once I didn't know if I even knew what love was…but I do."

His dramatic eyes glowed with an inner fire that held her captive.

"Love is what I feel every time I look at you. Touch you." His voice broke. "I was nothing till I met you. I'd *be* nothing without you." He brought her hand to his lips and pressed a tender kiss to the knuckle. "I love you, Red."

Happy beyond measure, she whispered, "Oh, Ty."

"I love you." He repeated, then sealed his vow with a tender kiss.

He eased them apart and cleared his throat before

speaking. "What do you have to do today?"

She half-heartedly moved back to the armoire and pulled out her clothes. "I promised Sarah I would ride over and visit. Henry said yesterday she is worried sick about us. With the baby so close, she can't leave." She didn't bother with the screen as she quickly dressed in jeans and shirt. "I'll go visit her first, then into town to see if Leo has sent any other messages and pick up a couple of things Lupe needs. Should be back by late afternoon."

"You taking the wagon?"

She sat on the edge of the bed and pulled on her boots. "Take too long. Make better time on Midnight."

He stood awkwardly with her. "Dammit. I hate like hell letting you go off alone like this."

Too happy to be nettled by his *letting-you-go* phrase, she kept silent.

"And don't go getting pissed at me cause I said I was *letting* you go. You know what I mean."

Her face split into a wide grin. "I know you love me." She kissed his nose. "So I'm giving you that one."

"You are, huh?"

His devastating smile made her pulse race.

"I am." She headed for the door before she changed her mind and stayed.

"Be careful."

"I will. Back soon."

Her feet never touched the ground as she floated down the hall.

Ty leaned on the bannister at the foot of the steps, brow beaded with sweat, breathing labored.

Okay, maybe I'm not as strong as I thought. Evidently making passionate love to his wife – several times – didn't mean his stamina returned in full. His injured leg ached like a bitch and his shoulder throbbed because he used his arm for balance on this adventure. Even though he took the stairs slowly, the effort drained him.

"Señor, Ty! Are you all right?"

Lupe's concerned question brought him upright. Sort of. "I reckon I've been better." He didn't protest as she assisted him to the nearest chair. "Guess I'm not as strong as I thought."

"Where are you headed? Do you want breakfast?"

"Maybe later. I wanted to check on Rafe…soon as I get my wind back."

A few minutes later, he sat in a chair by his father-in-law's bed, a cup of coffee in his hand.

"So glad to see you up, Tyler. I been worried 'bout you." Face etched with concern, Rafe stared at him.

"Glad to be up, sir."

"Emma told me your memory's back."

"Well, not all of it. I still have gaps here and there, but yeah, most of it's back." He avoided meeting Rafe's gaze as heat edged up his cheeks with the memory of their night of passion. *Glad I ain't shaved yet so he can't tell.*

"What about gettin' shot?"

He shook his head and tasted the coffee. "I remember leaving Emma – " The heat returned to his face and he looked toward the window. "And riding back toward the herd. Next thing I remember is seeing her walk in the room after I got here." *And bastard that I am, I didn't remember her.*

Rafe cleared his throat. "She doesn't blame you, you know. For not remembering."

"How can a man forget the woman he loves?" Ty winced as the words left his mouth but didn't regret them. Rafe had a right to know the feelings of the man who married his daughter.

"I knew I was right about you all along."

Rafe's self-satisfied smile rubbed against Ty's nerves like gravel on bare feet. "Would you have done it?" He didn't bother to explain the question.

Rafe sighed and leaned back against the pillows supporting him. "No. Despite what she thought, and most likely still thinks."

"She said it's in your will…"

His mouth tightened into a straight line. "The thought of her being left alone, with no one to look out for her…at the mercy of scoundrels like Walker from now on, just tore me up inside." His eyes sharp and compelling, he stared at Ty. "It was a threat, son, just a threat. I would never force her to marry against her will."

A brief, painful flash seared through his brain but disappeared before he could grasp it. He refocused his attention on Rafe, whose pale blue eyes glowed with conviction.

"Someday, you'll understand how far a father will go for his child." A coughing spell ended the conversation.

Ty sat helplessly by and waited for it to pass.

At length, it did and the old man sank against the pillows, energy exhausted.

"Can I do anything for you, sir?"

Eyes closed, the old man shook his head. "Just take care

of my girl."

"You have my word."

"I would've been a good grandpa," he whispered as he drifted off to sleep.

CHAPTER
Thirty-Four

"I KNEW IT!" SARAH CLAPPED HER HANDS IN GLEE AS SHE faced Emma. "I knew it would work out!"

Emma didn't want to discourage her friend's happiness by airing her doubts of a few days ago.

Today, she believed in miracles.

"Yeah, well, it was slow coming, but it finally did."

"Tell me again how he said he loved you." Ever the romantic, Sarah's eyes glistened with tears of joy, as Emma repeated the gist of the story.

"I'm so happy for you, Emma."

"I'm happy for me, too." She reached for her friend's hand. "How are you? Henry said yesterday you've been poorly."

Sarah flinched. "Kicked me again." She placed Emma's hand over her swollen middle. "Feel this."

Emma stared at her hand in amazement as she felt the

movement beneath. "Oh my goodness! Does that happen often?"

"Often enough lately." She laughed. "And judging by the smile you've been wearing since you got here, I'm thinking you'll be finding out for yourself soon enough."

Emma jerked her hand back, petrified at the thought of a life growing inside *her*. "How can you be so calm about this, Sarah?"

Immediately, she regretted the question for her friend's bright smile wavered then drifted away.

"We waited…we prayed for a child for over four years." Anguish clouded her face. "I thought something was wrong with me."

Sadness filled Emma's soul as she gripped her friend's cool hands and listened to her recount the heartbreaking end of her first pregnancy.

"I still think about her…so tiny." Her voice cracked. She looked up with anxious eyes. "Everything will be fine. I went much longer this time. God won't do that to me again." She spoke with a quiet, desperate firmness. "He won't."

Miserable she unwittingly brought up such a painful event, Emma sought a way to bring the joy back to Sarah's face. "I told him what you said about the hornet's nest."

Sarah's mouth dropped open and her brows shot up in surprise. Half-laughing, half-crying, she squeaked. "You didn't!"

Emma lifted one shoulder. "I was nervous, and we were, well…it just slipped out."

Sarah dropped back in the chair, laughing so hard she shook. "Wh-what did he say?"

"Nothing. Just kinda looked at me like maybe he wanted

to laugh or something."

"Oh my God! How will I ever look him in the face again?"

The laughter stopped abruptly and Emma feared the worst.

"What is it? Should I get Henry?"

"What else did you tell him?" Sarah's face paled. "We talked about a lot of…stuff."

More than I'll ever admit to. "I'm surprised I remember that much." Emma jumped up and marched to the mantel, moving the items on it around. "I was…a little preoccupied at the time."

Her admission brought another burst of laughter from Sarah and Emma relaxed.

The visit ended much too soon and Emma left with a promise to return as soon as possible.

The ride to town took longer than she anticipated due to flooded areas from the recent storm, but she made it at last.

She stopped at the telegraph office first and discovered a message just arrived from Leo.

"Afternoon, Miss Emma," gushed Otis Appleby, the operator. "You must be into mind readin' since this just came for you." He handed the slip of paper to her and practically danced as he related the contents. "Leo's gonna be home in about three days with them fancy cows you bought. I wonder what his surprise is?"

She took the paper and gritted her teeth. By sundown, the whole town would know all about it. She could almost hear the gossipmongers asking *what's that crazy Marshall girl up to now?* "Thank you, Mr. Appleby." She turned to leave.

"What's a Here Ford?"

She pasted on a tolerant smile. "A cow. And it's

pronounced her-fered."

"Whatcha gonna do with 'em?"

"Teach 'em to sing." She didn't look back as she left to pay a quick visit to Mabel at the General Store.

The cowbell over the door clanked as she entered.

"Be right there," Mabel's deep voice resonated from the backroom.

"It's just me, Mae, take your time."

She walked around the store, enjoying the smells of tobacco and coffee mixed with the aroma of leather and gun oil. She picked up the items Lupe requested, then paused at the jars filled with hard candies. In their short time together, she discovered Ty had a sweet tooth, so she picked out several for him.

"Emma!" The shopkeeper emerged from the back room wiping her hands on the apron circling a full waist. She wrapped her arms around Emma and squeezed hard before stepping back to look at her. "Well, I'd say marriage certainly agrees with you."

Heat flooded her face and she looked down. "It's okay."

A hearty laugh accompanied another hug. "Yes, it is. Now, tell me all about that man of yours. How is he?"

The hour passed much too quickly. "I do declare, child, you have had one hell of a row to hoe in such a short period of time."

Emma couldn't argue with her comment.

"And he has no idea who shot him?"

"None."

"Who on earth would want to hurt him?"

Who indeed?

Mable moved behind the counter and wrapped Emma's

purchases. She reached for the candy Emma selected, then added a couple of extra pieces. "After all he's been through, a little sweetening up won't hurt none. Oh…almost forgot." She reached behind her and retrieved a small package. "I saved you some of that new rose scented soap you like so well."

"How thoughtful. Thank you, Mae."

The older woman came back around the counter and embraced Emma again. "I never seen you look so happy." She pulled up the edge of her apron and swiped at her eyes. "I swear it just makes my heart sing." She straightened and gave her a playful shove toward the door. "You best get on home. Don't want your man kept waitin.'"

"Thank you, Mae. For everything." She swallowed past the lump in her throat. "You've been a good friend."

She rubbed Emma's shoulder. "As have you. Now go. It's gonna be dark before you get home."

She stowed the packages in her saddlebag and reached for Midnight's reins.

"Well, if it isn't the lovely Mrs. Roundtree."

Her foot froze in the stirrup at the sound of Hank Walker's voice.

CHAPTER
Thirty Five

WALLY'S MAKESHIFT CRUTCH THUMPED AS TY PACED across the porch. "Where the hell is she?" he muttered to the darkening sky. "I never should've let her go alone."

"If she didn't make it to the Owens place, someone would have told you before now."

Wally's quiet statement interrupted his self-bashing.

"So I reckon the best place to start looking is in town."

Ty didn't hesitate. "She'll be mad as hell at both of us, but yeah, go find her."

Wally's departure left Ty with nothing to occupy his mind except visions of all that might have happened.

What if she didn't make it to Sarah's? What if something happen in town? Thoughts of her being caught alone by Walker had him shaking in impotent anger. *I should have gone with her. I promised to protect her! Instead, I'm useless!*

He slammed the crutch against the porch post and promptly found his ass on the rough floor when the crutch snapped in half. "Dammit!"

He threw the remaining piece across the yard as Lupe and José ran to the door. "Señor, Ty! What has happened?"

He huffed out a breath, shame flooding his cheeks with heat. "Help me to the chair, José. Please."

Once settled, he grimaced. "I broke the crutch."

"Wally made two," said José, "He was not sure of the strength of his work."

"His work is fine. I'm the problem."

"She will be fine, Señor," said Lupe. "She is smart and strong, whatever has delayed her, she will be fine."

He didn't share her optimism.

"Shall I bring you some coffee?"

"No thank you, Lupe."

She nodded to her husband, then went back inside.

"I'll get the other crutch," said José, "It is in the barn."

He didn't reply as the older man walked away. *Where the hell is she?* He took a deep breath and tried to calm his raging anxiety. *Please God. Let her be all right.*

The screen door opened and he turned to see Lupe standing there, a steaming cup in her hand. "I added a touch of whiskey. It will help."

"Thank you."

She paused. "Your heart knows she is all right. Just like hers knew you lived." Then she turned and disappeared inside.

Did his heart know something he didn't? He lowered the cup to his lap and closed his eyes, visualizing her as she appeared when he woke this morning. Hair mussed, emerald eyes radiant, wearing nothing but his shirt…and that smile. Did she have any idea how captivating she appeared to him at that moment? He doubted it. Unlike other beautiful women he had known, she didn't seem aware of her beauty; didn't use it as a tool, which made it all the more alluring. *Something's wrong, but she's alive.*

The thought, more like a voice in his head, made him jump. "She's alive."

He sat back in his chair and took a sip of the whiskey-laced coffee.

And waited.

An hour later, the calm brought on by the spiked drink disappeared. "Where are they?" he muttered to the darkness, then tensed when the sound of an approaching rider reached his ears.

One horse. Not two.

His heart rate escalated as he grabbed the crutch and hobbled to the edge of the porch waiting for the visitor to come into view.

"Found her, Boss," said Wally as he approached the porch and dismounted.

"What the hell happened?" he snapped as Emma slid to the ground and limped up the steps.

"I think Midnight has spent way too much time with Diablo." She walked up to him and grinned. "I was distracted when something spooked her and she tossed me. Again. I walked a couple of miles before Wally found me." She exhaled loudly and looked toward the barn. "I figured the stupid horse beat me here and you sent him to find me."

He noted the dirty face and disheveled hair. "Are you hurt?"

"I'm fine. As you well know, I've been tossed before."

"Dammit, Red!"

His harsh voice made her take a step back.

"I've been going out of my mind! I *knew* I should never have let you go alone."

She bristled. "*Let* me? Now see here –"

Her retort ended when he dropped the crutch and pulled her roughly, almost violently to him even as his sore arm protested and a shudder ran through him. "Don't ever scare me like that again."

She pulled back slightly and met his steady gaze. "Ty, I'm all right." She caressed his cheek with one hand. "I'm sorry I worried you. I've been on my own for so long, I didn't… I'm sorry. Everything took longer than I thought, and then Midnight acted up."

As if on cue, a soft whiney announced the skittish horse's arrival.

"I'll get her to the barn," announced Wally, "and make sure she's not hurt."

"About time you got home," announced Lupe from the open doorway. "Supper is ready."

Ty couldn't stop shaking. "Is this what it was like for you?"

She nodded, eyes never leaving his.

He wrapped his arms around her again, more gentle this time, breathing in her scent as if it were a life-giving potion. "I don't want either of us to ever feel that way again."

Emma cast a sideways glance at Ty as they sat side-by-side

eating supper. His reaction to her tardiness unnerved her. She had no idea he would be so upset. *What will he do when I tell him about Walker?*

In an effort to delay the inevitable, she steered the conversation elsewhere. "Sarah has been so worried about you. I'm glad I had good news to tell her."

"When's the baby due again? I don't seem to recall."

"She said it could be anytime now but she thought probably a couple of weeks." Emma shook her head in wonder. "No idea how she can be so sure."

"Probably a female-thing," mumbled Ty around his last mouthful of potatoes. "Kinda like how horses and cows know when it's time."

For whatever reason, that struck her as funny and she chuckled. "I don't think I'll tell her you said she was like a cow."

He cast her a quizzical look, and frowned. "I didn't say she was like a cow."

Emma patted the hand resting beside hers on the table. "I know. It just sounded funny to me. Oh, I almost forgot." She reached in her shirt pocket and handed him Leo's message. "They should be home sometime next week."

Ty read the telegram, then handed it back. "Wonder what his surprise is?"

"I'm hoping the heifers are bred. Mr. Ralston said he thought they might be."

"That would be nice." He swiped his mouth with a napkin and placed it on the table. "I know you saw Walker in town. What happened?"

She jerked, then caught herself. "What makes you say that?"

He turned sideways in his chair and faced her. "It's a very small town. And you have talked about everything under the sun." He paused and fixed those all-seeing eyes on her. "Except what happened when you got there."

Lupe's entrance from the kitchen gave her a brief reprieve.

"José took these from the saddle bags."

Emma took the paper wrapped packages and placed them on the table. "Thank you, Lupe."

"Would you like more coffee, Señor Ty?"

"Not right now, thank you."

She nodded and left the room

"I know how you like sweets." Emma slid the treats toward him, carefully avoiding eye contact.

He glanced at it, then back to her. "Well?"

She picked up her fork then lay it back down, glancing at him. "I'm not trying to keep anything from you."

The scowl on his face said he disagreed.

She huffed, then turned and faced him. "Fine. I saw Walker in town. He spoke. I left."

His jaw muscles moved, but he remained silent.

She sighed. "It was outside the general store. I was about to leave when he walked up."

"And?"

"And nothing. Mable was standing there and all he said was something like nice to see you Mrs. Roundtree." There was more but she would not tell him tonight. *He stood much too close and licked his lips. His fingers touched the brim of his hat then inched forward.*

She blocked out the fear he instilled with his presence. He fed on fear and she would not give him the satisfaction. Not anymore.

"He offered to keep me company on the long ride home."

Ty stiffened.

"I told him to go to hell."

His face showed no reaction. "You did?"

"Yes. And frankly, it felt pretty damn good to do it." She rubbed her hands on her thighs. "I thought Mable would choke trying not to laugh."

"What did he do?"

"Walked away."

"He just walked off?" His voice carried a note of disbelief.

"Well, he mumbled something under his breath I didn't catch." *Liar. He said he liked his women to have spunk.* "I didn't hang around to ask him what."

After a moment, Ty shook his head, voice firm. "That's your last trip to town alone." He held up his hand to silence her protest. "You can holler and scream till your eyes bug out but you are *not* going anywhere alone again. Period." He raked his fingers through his hair and sighed. "Something's not right about him, Em. I'm not sure what it is but something's wrong and you're involved in it. Until I know you are out of danger, do as I say. Please."

She started to object to his decree, argue for her independence. She was not helpless after all; but one look at the gravity and concern in his expression and she swallowed her objection.

He loves me.

"Well, since you said, please…"

After a brief hesitation, one heavy brow lifted slightly, a smile edging up the corner of his mouth. "Damn. I was hoping you'd argue more…so we can make up."

She leaned toward him, hands sliding up his thighs.

"Oh, but I did argue," she whispered softly, "I hollered and screamed till my eyes bugged out. The fact that I did it all in my head means nothing."

The caress of his lips on hers set her body aflame.

Her hands slipped around his neck and she lost herself in the tenderness of the kiss.

"Don't forget – I won't always be so agreeable."

He pulled her in his lap. "I'm counting on it."

CHAPTER
Thirty-Six

"How was the ride?" Rafe's cheerful voice greeted Ty as he rode up to the porch.

"Good." He gave a soft laugh. "Better than yesterday. Didn't think I'd be so sore." The old rocker squeaked when sat beside his father-in-law.

"Well, it's only been a month or so since the accident. And you been abed most of the time."

"True. But I thought walking around would help more." Ty rocked slowly back and forth enjoying Rafe's company. "Fresh air and sunshine work wonders, don't they?"

"I haven't felt this good in months. Thanks for asking José to bring me out here," said Rafe as he adjusted the blanket around his knees. "I miss being outside."

"I was going crazy cooped up in the house. Figured you might feel the same."

"You're right. Looking out the window is fine, but bein'

out here, smellin' the air…there ain't nothin' like it."

Lupe brought them a cup of coffee and they sat in companionable silence for several minutes.

"What do you know about Herefords?" asked Rafe.

"Not much. They originally came from some place in England. Sude Ikard brought some back from up north a couple of years ago. Texas Fever got most of the first group, so he bought some more. He thinks they'll replace the Longhorn."

"Yeah, that's what Ralston told me last year. I never really gave much thought to buyin' any. What do you think about it?"

"Emma's smart. She wouldn't have done it if she didn't think it was the right decision."

"Did she talk to you about it?"

Ty chose his words carefully. The last thing he wanted was for Rafe to think he might not support his wife's decision. "Wasn't necessary. This is her ranch. She'll do what's best for it and didn't need to discuss it with me first." He placed his empty cup on the floor. "But if she had, I would have encouraged her to do it."

Rafe's brow crinkled in thought. "Why?"

"Well, they're a hearty breed, more adaptable to open ranges, fatten quicker, and the meat is supposedly better."

Rafe smiled. "I thought you didn't know much about 'em."

Ty lifted a shoulder. "I've met Sude Ikard. All he talks about is the future of Herefords in Texas." His gaze drifted past the yard to the pasture behind the barn. "The grazing is good here, plenty of water, winters can be hard but not like up north." He turned to face the older man. "Any decision she makes will be because she's a rancher's daughter – and you taught her well."

Rafe smiled and leaned back in his chair. "She's quite a gal ain't she?"

"Yes, sir, she is for a fact."

Emma edged away from the door and swiped at the tears stinging her eyes. When she first over-heard Rafe ask Ty about the Herefords, she prepared to barge out there and defend her decision. Thankfully, she refrained. Her father wasn't upset about the cattle and Ty said she did the right thing. The two most important men in her life thought she was special and that made her all emotional.

She sniffled as she sat down and focused on the paperwork in front of her. Leo would arrive soon with the new stock and she couldn't wait to find out if the heifers were bred. If so, the calves would drop before winter set in, and if they did as well as she anticipated, they would add to the herd next year. Thoughts of the white-faced cattle filling the range made her smile.

"I know it's not paperwork putting that smile on your face."

Ty's voice held a trace of amusement.

"Maybe I was thinking about you."

He sauntered into the room and took the chair in front of the desk. "A man can only dream."

"How was the ride? Wally didn't push too hard, did he?"

"Every day is better than the one before. And no, your nurse maid didn't push."

His terse comment widened her smile. "You won't let me go anywhere alone, so turnabout is fair play."

"It's been well over a month since the accident and I've been walking without the crutch all week."

"I know, but Diablo is so unpredictable. I just feel better when someone is with you."

"So, what were you so deep in thought about when I walked in?"

All of sudden, she was nervous about the topic and looked everywhere but at him. "Well, um, I – I was thinking about the new cattle."

He stared a moment, then leaned forward in his chair. "Emma, you've got a rancher's head on your shoulders. Buying those cattle was the right thing to do."

She nibbled her lower lip. "I made the deal for them before you came here, but I still should have mentioned it to you."

"Emma. Look at me."

She took a breath and met his steady gaze.

"I grew up on a small plantation in Georgia. I know about hard work, managing crops, and building things. We had cattle and horses, but our yields were the main focus. I've learned a lot about ranching since the war but I'm no expert. You are." He sat back in his chair. "Anytime you want to bounce something off me, or want my opinion on anything, I'm all ears. But you have the final say on anything pertaining to this ranch."

Even though she overhead him say something similar earlier, having him state it to her face was beyond exhilarating and her cheerfulness returned. "Thank you."

"You're welcome. Now…I'm assuming you're going to want to keep them in the corral for a bit after they get here?"

They spent the next half hour discussing accommodations for the new arrivals and other ranch business. It was wonderful to be able to discuss the inner workings of Twin Oaks with him. While he was bull headed at times, like not wanting her to go anywhere alone, he was also intelligent, supportive, and eager to learn and he possessed an off-beat sense of humor that matched her own.

He laughed at himself without rancor – like last night when he was so sore from his ride, every muscle hurt. It was one of those nights where they didn't make love. Instead, they fell asleep wrapped in each other's arms, which was emotionally satisfying in itself. She recalled the warmth of his skin against hers, the touch of his calloused hand on her arm, the brush of his lips on her brow. Happiness and contentment filled her. *I love this man. With every fiber of my being, I love him.*

It took a moment to realize he stopped in mid-sentence and watched her, his gaze soft and tender as a caress.

"What?"

"You're wearing that look again."

She arched a brow. "What look?"

He moved around the desk and pulled her up, hands cupping her face. "The one that says kiss me. Now." His lips brushed hers lightly, then covered her mouth.

She met his kiss eagerly, reveled in the gentleness of his touch, drowning in the sweet ecstasy it inflicted.

At length, he pulled back, gulping air before he placed a soft kiss on her forehead. "I better get out of here while I still can."

He grabbed his hat off the desk. "I'm going to take another ride, see if I can work out more of this soreness before tonight."

The look he gave her sent a rush of heat to her lower body.

It took a while for her heart rate to slow and concentration on work to return.

⭐ ⭐ ⭐

Three days later, Emma rode up to the front of the house and dismounted, delighted to see her father sitting on the front porch again. It was so hard to believe how much he improved each day. Just yesterday, Doc said maybe he was wrong and it wasn't consumption after all, but a prolonged case of pneumonia.

"How's Sarah today?"

"Good. She thinks the baby will be coming any time now."

"No problems?"

She shook her head. "I told Ty I didn't need for Wally to accompany me again, but he won't hear of it."

"Don't get mad, Emma Rose. He's concerned. That's all."

"I know. I just don't think I need a babysitter every time I go there. It's only an hour each way."

Rafe looked as though he was going to say something, then pointed off to the east. "They're here."

They watched in silence as Leo and two other hands brought the cows down the lane toward the corral.

"Still don't see why he didn't send at least one of the boys back. One man can handle three head."

Rafe's snippy comment caused Emma to bite back a smile. Her father was back. "I'm going over there. Think you can make it?"

He shook his head. "I'll wait for José or Tyler to help me. I can get by without the chair around the house, but that might be pushing it."

She gave him a quick kiss on the cheek, then dashed off toward the corral.

"Howdy, Miss Emma," said Leo as they herded the white

faced cows through the open gate where water and food awaited them.

"I didn't expect you for another day or two." She went to the fence and stepped on the bottom rail, arms draped over the top. "You made great time."

He nodded. "They trailed really good. Didn't have any trouble out of 'em at all." He dismounted and looped the reins over the fence, then reached in his pocket and handed her an envelope. "It's the bill of sale and the draft for the herd, minus the cost of the new stock."

She nodded and stuffed it in her back pocket. "They really are beautiful, aren't they?"

He looked at her and ducked his head, cheeks a bright red. "Yes, ma'am, they sure are."

"What about the heifers? Are they bred?" She gifted him with a bright smile. "Was that your surprise?"

He shuffled his feet, then removed his hat. "No ma'am. Uh, what with losing your husband and all, and well, your Pa, too…" his voice trailed off and he turned to his horse, retrieving something from his saddlebag. "Well, I thought you might need some cheering up." He held a small, crudely wrapped package in his hands.

Emma dropped down from the fence and looked at Leo, but didn't reach for the package. "I didn't lose my husband."

His brow puckered. "But he went in the water…we couldn't find him."

"As you can see, I am still here."

Leo whirled at the sound of Ty's voice, his face contorting briefly, then becoming unreadable.

"You ain't dead."

CHAPTER
Thirty-Seven

Ty knew all along Leo had feelings for Emma, but it wasn't until that brief moment before his expression became closed he realized the depth of those feelings. The cowhand was pissed.

Ty stood beside Emma, placing one arm around her waist. "Emma refused to give up. It took a couple of days, but she found me." He smiled down at his wife. "And brought me home."

Emma returned his look of affection. "My heart knew you were alive."

Ty pulled her closer, his intent not to hurt Leo further, but to firmly establish his place in Emma's life – just in case the younger man had any doubts.

Leo's jaw clenched, but his face remained unreadable as he stuffed the package back in the saddlebags.

Emma looked at Ty, her expression asking a question she

didn't voice. A minute shake of his head told her, *let it go*.

"They made the trip in fine shape, Leo," said Ty in an effort to get back on solid ground. "Y'all did a good job."

"Yeah," he mumbled, "it was only three head and they had some trail experience so we made good time." He turned back and cast a quick look at Emma before focusing his attention on Ty. "The larger one is bred. Probably drop the end of September maybe early October."

Emma clapped her hands in glee. "Wonderful!" She turned and climbed over the fence. "I have to look at them up close."

"Careful, Miss Emma," said Leo, "the bull ain't mean, but he sometimes gets cranky."

If she heard him, she gave no indication as she cautiously approached the cows to scratch their white heads, and run her hands over their sleek bodies.

Ty was about to join her when José rolled Rafe out to the corral.

Leo's face registered shock which quickly turned to a smile that never quite made it to his eyes. "Mr. Rafe! You sure are a sight for sore eyes." He reached out and shook the old man's hand.

"Welcome home, boy. Good to see you, too."

Leo shook his head. "To be honest, sir, I didn't expect to see you at all."

The older man's laugh was rusty, but pleased. "Kinda had my doubts, too, for a while, but looks like I might be around a bit longer."

"Doc seems to think maybe it wasn't consumption after all," declared Ty. "Just pneumonia that hung on longer than normal."

"I ain't completely recovered yet, but I'm better ever'day. Can even walk around the house some on my own now."

Leo's cheeks reddened and he looked around. "Well, I best get my horse took care of. I gave Miss, uh, your wife, the bill of sale and the bank draft." He turned and pulled his horse toward the barn.

Ty decided this wasn't the time to ask if he still intended to leave as he said before the drive. "Want a closer look?" he asked Rafe.

"Go ahead. I'll look from here."

"Okay." Ty climbed the fence and joined his wife.

Supper that night was a cheerful affair. Rafe sat at his place at the head of the table, Ty on his right and Emma beside him.

"I plan to keep them in the corral for the next few days," said Emma, "see how they do, make sure we don't have any problems, then move them to the north pasture maybe next week." Her brows pulled together and she looked at her father. "Do you think the other bulls, particularly the Longhorns, might go after Big Red?"

"Big Red?" Questioned Ty. "You named them?"

She nodded briskly. "The pregnant one is Maggie and the younger one is Daisy."

Rafe chuckled, but made no comment.

Ty smiled at the seriousness of her expression.

"They're special. They needed names." She took a quick bite of her stew. "Oh, and tomorrow, I'm going back over to Sarah's for a few days. She said today it's almost time and wants me to be there."

"I'll go with you," said Ty tersely.

"Who will look after Big Red and the girls?"

"You're not going anywhere alone. Period. End of discussion."

"Ty – "

"Someone tried to kill me, Em, and failed. They could try again any time or worse, use you to get to me."

Her eyes widened and she gasped.

Evidently, that thought never occurred to her. "Until I am convinced there is no cause for concern, you don't go anywhere alone. I'll ride over with you, and then come back and check on you in a couple of days."

The hard set of her jaw told him an argument loomed, so he softened his demand. "Please."

After a brief pause, she looked at him, concern shimmering in her eyes. "Do you really think whoever shot at you might try again?"

He didn't want to frighten her, but he also wanted to make sure she understood the seriousness of the situation. "That's just it, I don't know. Until I do, you go nowhere alone."

After a brief hesitation, she huffed. "Just because you said please don't mean I'm happy about being ordered around."

The cheerful atmosphere returned, and he breathed a sigh of relief.

"It will give me a chance to say hello in person. I haven't been by since I got my memory back."

"Fine," she muttered. "We leave after morning chores."

He hid his grin behind a sip of coffee. She may be miffed now, but come bedtime, he'd make her happy to have him around.

CHAPTER
Thirty-Eight

"**A**REN'T YOU GLAD YOU LET ME TAG ALONG?**"**

Emma had difficulty concentrating as she lay beside him under the shade of a towering pine, her body still shuddering from the power of her release. "Maybe."

Laughter vibrated through the cheek resting on his bare chest.

"We need to get going, though."

She noted his voice didn't sound too happy with that idea. "Just five more minutes." She raked her fingers through the tight curls on his chest, lightly scraping across one nipple before angling lower.

He hissed in a breath and pressed down on her wandering hand. "Enough or Sarah's baby will arrive before we get there."

Reluctantly, they separated and were soon on their way to the Owens ranch where Henry greeted them at the door.

"Thank God you're here!" He pulled Emma inside. "She's been asking for you. She thinks the baby will be here soon and I have no idea what to do."

Emma barely controlled the urge to tell him he wasn't alone.

"Do you need me to ride into town for the doctor?" asked Ty.

He shook his. "I sent one of the boys already."

Ty looked at Emma. "Em? What do you need me to do?"

The question broke through the panic building inside her head. She struggled to maintain a cheery demeanor. "Know how to deliver a baby?" *Please say yes, please say yes.*

"Uh…no."

"Then I guess just keep Henry company." She headed up the stairs.

"I have hot water ready when you need it."

What the hell will I need hot water for?

A loud moan from the room on the right sent a shiver up Emma's spine as she entered and found Sarah clutching the rails at the head of bed, face contorted in pain as another spasm gripped her.

With no clue what to do, Emma sat on the side of the bed and used a cloth on the nearby table to wipe her friend's brow.

"Boy," Sarah grimaced at last, "that was a dandy." Yellow-gold hair, damp with perspiration, clung to ashen cheeks, but her blue eyes sparkled with happiness and a tired smile graced her face. "I'm pretty sure the baby will be here before Doc arrives." She looked intently at Emma. "I can't lose my baby, Emma. You have to help me."

Emma was too shocked to respond at first, and then she

squeaked, "I know about pulling calves, not babies."

Sarah gritted her teeth and groaned as another contraction wracked her body. When it passed, she drew in deep gulps of air and looked at her. "It's not all that different with babies."

Emma flinched, then gasped. "Oh my God! I have to put a rope around its feet and pull it out?"

Sarah's laughter was strained. "Good Lord, girl. I could write a book about stuff you don't know."

Emma couldn't argue with her comment, so remained silent.

"I don't remember much about the first time since I was so sick, but this is what Mable said."

Emma listened with rapt attention as she learned the basics of childbirth, all the while praying God would help her and she didn't pass out.

The spasms came closer together and with each one, Emma's own anxiety mounted. *What if something goes wrong? What if I do something wrong? I couldn't bear it!*

"It's time!" cried Sarah, "it's time!"

Emma followed the instructions as best she could, and soon held the newborn in her hands. "It's a girl!"

"She's not crying!" wailed Sarah, "she has to cry!"

Panicky and unsure of how to accomplish that part, she did what she would if it were a newborn calf: cleared her mouth, then held her up by her tiny ankles and tapped her on the back. When that didn't work right away, she swung her lightly side to side, then popped her on the butt.

The baby's shrill cry, mixed with the happy cries of mother and makeshift-midwife, filled the room.

Now I know what the hot water is for.

★ ★ ★

At Emma's instruction, Henry and Ty cautiously entered the room.

Sarah's face beamed as she looked at her husband. "Come meet your daughter."

Emma worked hard not to cry again at the sight of Henry carefully holding the blanket-wrapped babe, his mouth curved with tenderness and wonder. "She's beautiful," he whispered, "just like her mother."

Ty slid an arm around Emma's waist and she leaned into him, surprised to note her shaky knees wouldn't support her.

"Congratulations you two," said Ty. "Do you have a name yet?"

Sarah looked at Emma, then back to Henry. "I'd like to name her Abigail Rose, after my mother," she looked at Emma again, love etched in the smile she wore. "And my sister by choice."

Henry looked down at his daughter. "Hello, Abigail Rose. I'm your father."

The tears started again in earnest.

CHAPTER
Thirty-Nine

Ty gazed at Emma over the breakfast table. "Something bothering you? You've been unusually quiet this morning."

She nibbled her lower lip, then huffed out a breath. "I didn't know childbirth was so…painful."

Uh-oh.

He put his cup down and focused on her. "And?"

She met his steady gaze. "Sarah said this morning she didn't even remember the pain now, which seems kinda far-fetched to me." Her cheeks turned a lovely shade of pink. "What she said reminded me of the first time…" She straightened her back and continued. "She told me afterwards it was all worth it and she'd do it again."

It suddenly occurred to him, he had no idea how she felt about actually having a child, though he told her up front, he wanted one.

He needed to know if she would have his child. "Do you want children, Em?"

Her hands were hidden under the table but he guessed them to be clasped tightly together. "Well, I admit that yesterday, I had my doubts."

"And today?" He held his breath as he waited. He wanted a child in the worst way, but if she didn't…

A shivering breath preceded her answer. "When I saw Henry hold little Abby, the look on his face…" She swallowed and her jaw clenched. "I pictured you like that, holding our child…" Her laugh was dubious. "I'll probably be a mess the whole time, but, yes I do."

He released a heavy sigh. "So do I."

Her silky voice held a healthy dose of sensuality and humor. "Well, if we don't have one soon, it won't be for lack of trying."

Delight surged through him. "I love you, Red."

"I love you, too," she replied softly.

"Any coffee left?" asked Henry as he stumbled into the kitchen. "I'm dying."

"On the stove," said Emma, "and some bacon and eggs."

He grabbed a cup and joined them at the table, yawning fiercely before taking a drink. "Abby was awake every two hours last night." He turned to Emma. "Is that normal?"

She snorted. "How should I know?"

"You're a woman."

His matter-of-fact statement apparently struck her as funny since a gentle laugh rippled through the air.

"Yeah, well, you could write a book on what I don't know about being a woman." She laughed again, a happy, musical laugh that made the men smile in return.

Ty hated to leave Emma, but knew he needed to get back. "When do you want me to come get you? Tomorrow, the next day?"

She looked at Henry. "When will your housekeeper be back?"

"Tomorrow." He shook his head. "She's going to be upset about missing the birth, but her mother was sick so she needed to go."

"Day after tomorrow just in case she's late." She grinned at Henry. "You'll be tired of bacon and eggs by then, since that's all I know how to cook."

"But you make great coffee." He refilled his cup and left the room.

★ ★ ★

Ty reached the ranch shortly after lunch and found Rafe sitting in his rocker on the porch. "Was worried something went wrong. I expected you back yesterday."

"Everything's fine." He looped the reins around the post and stepped on the porch. "Sarah had a little girl late yesterday. Emma's staying till the housekeeper gets back."

"They doing all right?"

"Yeah. Doc said everything's fine." He took the chair beside him, wondering how to ask the question buzzing around his head like a fly for the last two days. Elbows on his knees, he clasped his hands in front.

"Out with it, Boy," said Rafe as he watched him closely. "Whatever is stuck in your craw, just spit it out."

"A while back, you told me you never intended to go through with willing the ranch away if Emma didn't marry;

it was all a bluff."

Rafe stiffened and his voice sparked with edginess. "That's right."

Ty met the old man's direct gaze. "I saw the paper the night we decided to marry. Frankly, it was part of the reason I did it." He shook his head. "She was devastated. I had to do something."

The older man leaned forward, face drawn tight. "What the hell are you talking about? Saw what?"

"The amendment to the will. I didn't actually remember seeing it until a couple of days ago." He rubbed his hands across his thighs. "I didn't trust my recollection, so yesterday, before we left, I looked at it again."

"I don't know what the hell you saw, Tyler, but I never made any changes to my will!"

Ty studied him a moment. "Be right back."

A few minutes later, he returned and handed him the envelope with the will inside.

Rafe barely glanced at the will when he saw the second document. "What's this?"

"An amendment to your will setting out the stipulations for Emma to marry." Ty barely contained the anger in his voice.

"I don't know anything about this and for damn sure I never signed it!" Rafe's face reddened and his breath came in rapid puffs.

Concern for the older man tempered Ty's anger. "Okay, okay...don't get worked up."

Rafe took a deep breath. "Where did you get this?"

"Emma showed it to me the night we decided to get married. Like I said, it was part of the reason for our decision."

"You married my girl for this ranch?" Rafe's voice shook with anger. "That's all she is to you?"

"Hell no!" Ty worked at control. "I told her no matter what happened between us, this is her place. Period. I wanted a wife and family. A home." He took a deep breath. "I still do."

Rafe sank back in the chair. "Thank God. I'd hate to have to make her a widow."

Ty let his remark slide as he processed a more vital question. *If he didn't sign it, who did? And why?* He reached for the document still clutched in the old man's hand. "Obviously, Walker wrote this up. The question is why? And who signed it?"

His frail shoulders drooped and his voice sounded tired. "When I got real bad, he was here one day talking about what happens to Emma when I'm gone. It made me think hard about things."

"And he suggested this?" He held up the paper.

He nodded. "More or less. He talked about her being left alone and how much work was involved in running this place, and how the men wouldn't work for her after I'm dead. Stuff like that." His cheeks reddened and he looked at Ty. "I know what you're thinking, boy, that I would force my girl to take someone she didn't want. But you're wrong." He blew out a heavy breath. "I reckon I went a bit too far doing that advertisement and all, but she wouldn't give the time of day to any man around here." His face grew red and a short coughing spell interrupted his comments.

"Need some water?"

"Rather have whiskey."

Ty raised a brow, but went inside and returned with a glass.

Rafe downed the contents, sputtered once, and then looked at Ty, his blue eyes clear and direct. "I never told him to do that. Never."

Ty believed him, so the burning questions remained: Who did? And why?

Rafe cleared his throat. "What now?"

"I'm going to talk to him," said Ty firmly, "If I don't like his answers, I'll talk to the sheriff."

He caught a slight movement from the corner of his eye and turned to see Leo standing at the edge of the porch, expression unreadable. *How much did he hear? Does it matter?*

"Thought I heard someone ride up." There was an edge to his voice he couldn't hide. "Want me to take care of your horse?"

Ty's instincts went on full alert. "No, thank you. I'll take care of him later."

A curt nod and he turned toward the barn.

"You ain't going to see him alone," stated Rafe in a tense, clipped voice that forbade discussion.

"If Walker's behind this, he broke the law. Which begs the question, how many others has he broken?"

"All the more reason for you to take someone with you." He looked around. "Take Wally or Leo."

Ty's first instinct was to refuse, but going alone was risky. For whatever reason, he didn't trust Leo, probably because he knew how the young cowhand felt about Emma. Wally was young, but solid, and stuck with Emma when she needed someone and the reason they kept him on as a full-time hand afterwards.

"I'll take Wally. Where is he?"

"He went into town. José needed some supplies."

"I'll catch up to him there." He started for his horse and paused. "I think I'll put the papers back in the safe for now."

A few minutes later, he was ready to ride.

"Tyler."

He stopped at the old man's sharp call.

"Be careful."

He gave a curt nod and rode off.

The trip into town took less than an hour, but the good luck ended there. Walker was nowhere to be found, and the sheriff wasn't in his office.

A brief stop at the saloon to see if anyone knew when the sheriff would return proved fruitless as well. Wally was there talking to one of the working girls and he just nodded at the boy and left.

He didn't like not being able to finish this business, but it couldn't be helped. Disappointed, he got back on his horse and headed for home.

Diablo showed his displeasure at setting out again so soon by refusing to cooperate. If Ty wanted him to go left, he went right. If he urged him to go faster, he slowed down.

"You worthless piece of horseflesh!" grumbled Ty as he struggled to keep the unpredictable horse on the road. "I ought'a put you out of my misery."

On the heels of that outburst, Diablo suddenly reared and took off like the hounds of hell were after him. All Ty could do was hold on.

A mile or so later, the devil horse stopped so fast Ty nearly went flying over his head. The animal blew hard and his legs trembled.

Suddenly alarmed, Ty bent forward, rubbing the horses' sleek neck as he prepared to dismount. "Easy boy, easy.

What's wrong?"

The horse staggered slightly, throwing Ty off-balance and he slid to one side. Otherwise, the bullet that zipped past his ear might have killed him.

245

CHAPTER
Forty

"I THOUGHT YOU SAID Ty DIDN'T WANT YOU RIDING anywhere alone?"

Emma brushed off Sarah's concern with a wave of her hand. "I need to get home. Since your housekeeper came back early, now is a good time for me to go so I will be home before dark." She sat on the edge of the bed. "I'm so happy for you, Sarah. Abby is a beautiful child."

Her friend wrapped her hands around Emma's. "If you hadn't been here…." Her face lost a bit of its color and her voice trailed off.

"No ifs, Sarah. I *was* here and you told me what to do. Everything worked out fine, and now I have a beautiful niece by choice." *Even though I was scared out of my wits and had no idea what the hell I was doing.* She arched a brow. "Who knows, maybe one day you can return the favor."

Sarah laughed. "I hope so, Emma, I truly do!"

Henry entered with a food tray and Emma stood so he could place it on the bed. "Gertie is so upset over not being here, I fear she may over-feed us all."

Emma's mouth watered at the food-laden tray. "Beats the hell out of my bacon and eggs."

"Emma's riding back tonight." Sarah's proclamation held a note of censure.

"I'll go with you," said Henry, "just give me time to saddle up."

"Don't be ridiculous. Sarah needs you and I am perfectly capable of riding alone."

"I have no desire for your husband to kick my ass from here to sundown cause I let you ride out alone knowing full well he wouldn't like it." He smiled at Sarah. "Gertie will be worse than a mother hen." He placed a quick kiss on her brow. "I'll be back as soon as I can." Then he pointed a finger at Emma. "And *you* will not leave without me. Is that clear?"

She straightened and managed a pitiful salute. "Yes *sir!*"

Henry chuckled. "Poor Ty. I'll be ready in fifteen minutes."

True to his word, Henry waited outside for her. "Just for the record, and so I can tell your husband I said so, you should wait at least until tomorrow."

"There is absolutely no reason for you to accompany me."

"Other than knowing Ty would insist."

She had the grace to be ashamed. "Well, yes, there is that."

"And it will be dark by the time we get there, so we need to get moving."

"I just hate taking you away from Sarah at a time like this."

"Sarah's fine. Let's go."

The sun touched the western horizon as they approached the entrance of Twin Oaks and Emma pulled to a stop. "This is far enough. I can make it from here without the boogeyman getting me."

"I'll see you all the way."

The stubborn set of his jaw reminded her of Ty and she grinned. "Henry, you have a wife and new baby daughter waiting at home." She pointed ahead. "We can see the house from here. You and I both know he's going to be upset and I don't think you want to be a party to that."

Henry looked toward the house, then back to Emma. "You got a point there." He blew out a breath. "I'll watch until you reach the yard."

"Fine." She took off at a gallop, turning when she reached the yard to wave him off.

Lamplight glowed through the parlor windows as she tied Midnight's reins to the post. She paused a moment at the door, contemplating putting her horse up first. She wanted to see Ty first, so she took a deep breath and mentally braced herself for the argument sure to erupt when she walked in, knowing he would be upset. Then she smiled. *Quarrels led to making up.*

She turned left toward the parlor and saw Rafe sitting in his chair by the mantel, an open book in his lap, talking with Leo, whose back was to the door.

"Where is it?" snapped Leo.

"Where is what?"

He whirled around at Emma's question, and she saw the gun in his hand. "Leo? What's going on?"

"Dammit! You're not supposed to be here!" He motioned with the gun to join her father and she complied.

"Papa? Are you all right?"

He patted the hand resting on his shoulder. "I'm fine."

"I ain't asking again old man. Where is it?"

Emma looked from her father to Leo. "Where is what?"

His jaw muscles moved, but Leo didn't answer.

"He wants the amendment to my will." Rafe faced the angry cowboy. "Ty has it. He's taking it to the sheriff."

Emma stared at her father. "Why on earth would Ty take it to the sheriff?"

Footsteps in the hallway made her heart jump. *Oh no! Lupe!*

Leo quickly holstered his gun and turned as she entered.

"More coffee – Señora, I did not know you were home. Have you eaten?"

"Yes, I have, thank you." She endeavored to keep her voice light. "Why don't you go on home? I'll take care of anything left in the kitchen."

She smiled brightly. "*Si*, I will do that. My José has been feeling ill today. There is fresh coffee on the stove. I will see you in the morning."

Leo pulled his pistol again and tilted his head toward the kitchen, presumably listening for the back door to shut. His voice was calm, his gaze steady as he looked at Rafe. "You're one tough ole buzzard."

"Thank you," said Rafe, voice heavy with sarcasm.

"If you'd just died like you was supposed to, everything would have worked out fine."

"Leo!" Emma stared at the young man she once considered a friend and realized he was a stranger.

He stepped forward, gun steady despite the nervous twitch in his face. "I would have done anything for you."

Emma stared, afraid to speak.

"I would have made you happy," he said without inflection as he adjusted the gun in his hand.

She eased herself between Leo and her father. "I don't know what's going on but I'm sure we can figure this out."

"Yeah," he said coolly, "we'll figure it out."

Emma struggled for a way out. *Where is Ty?* "I had no idea of your feelings, Leo, or I would have done things differently."

"You never even looked at me except to give me orders."

His voice, flat and devoid of emotion, terrified her more than rage.

"That's not true. I value our friendship."

"Friendship," he spat the word out like rotten fruit. "I loved you." The gun wobbled in his hand. "Let's just sit tight till Walker gets here."

Emma paled. Of course, Walker drew up all her father's legal papers, so he would be the one who drew up the amendment. *But why did he want it back?*

"I don't understand why you would go to all this trouble to get a document that is essentially useless since I married before the deadline and my father is still alive."

"Because I never saw that document," snapped Rafe, "much less signed it."

"You never…" His words bounced around in her head, the implications mounting. "If you didn't…"

"Then there wasn't any need for you to get married, was there?" taunted Leo. "But we can fix that, too."

Ty struggled to keep up the pace Walker set, furious with himself for getting caught off guard.

After the first two shots rang out, nothing more happened for a good twenty minutes, so he eased away from the big oak tree only to be knocked down by Walker whom he never even heard approach.

Now, here he was, tied up like a mustang, stumbling along behind his captor's horse. Twice he fell and the bastard simply pulled him along until he managed to stand on his own. He had no idea what happened to his own horse. Once he hit the ground, Diablo bolted.

Walker ignored his questions as he searched him for the document he wanted. Ty could only assume Leo was somehow involved and got word to Walker his ruse had been discovered.

In an effort to keep him away from the ranch, Ty told him he left it at the sheriff's office, which prompted a snort of derision and other hit with the butt of his gun.

By the time they arrived, he was exhausted, his fingers were numb from the tight rope binding his wrists, and his whole body hurt from being drug along the ground. He tasted sweat mixed with blood and dirt from a busted lip, and his barely healed wounds throbbed.

He bit back a curse when he saw Emma's horse tied out front. *Dammit! She can't do a thing I say!*

"Come along, Tyler. I'm sure your wife will be happy to see you." Walker took in his bedraggled appearance and laughed. "Then again, maybe not."

Fury nearly choked him as he glared at the lawyer. "You're a dead man."

A shadow of fear crossed the other man's eyes and

quickly vanished. "You forget who has the gun." He waved Ty's Colt in front of him as he backed up the steps, pulling the rope that bound his hands, causing it to dig deeper into his flesh. "Come along like a good boy."

Emma bolted from her chair when they entered the room only to be stopped by Leo, who held a gun on her. "Sit down!"

"Ty!" her face paled as she looked him over.

"I'm all right, Em." He turned his attention to the young cowhand. His temples throbbed with anger, but he spoke deliberately and with deadly calm. "If you so much as muss her hair I will kill you with my bare hands."

Leo backed up a little, then stood up straighter. "You ain't the one in charge now."

"Shut up, both of you," snapped Walker as he pushed Ty toward an empty chair. "Sit down." He turned his attention to Leo. "You damn fool. You had one job to do. One."

Leo shifted from one foot to the other. "He went in the water. I thought he was dead."

"Oh my God, Leo!" Emma's green eyes clawed at him like talons. "You shot Ty?"

"He was merely trying to save you from yourself."

Walker's patronizing tone made Ty's teeth ache. He glanced at his wife. *If looks could kill, asshole, you'd be buzzard bait right now.*

"Let's just get this over with, shall we." He focused on Emma. "What's the combination to the safe?"

"Go to hell."

"I do like a woman with spunk."

His smile was feral as he walked toward her and Ty came off the chair.

"Sit down, cowboy," he pulled the hammer back on

the pistol, "unless you want me to finish what that imbecile started."

"I already told Leo it ain't in the safe," said Rafe. "Tyler took it with him to town and gave it to the sheriff."

Ty kept his expression unreadable. Rafe lied. He knew Ty returned it to the safe before he left, so he could only guess the man was stalling.

"I tried to tell you," goaded Ty. "The sheriff will no doubt be stopping by any time to discuss the consequences of forgery with you."

"He went out to the Barker place this afternoon," said Walker, "and wasn't back when you were there." He smirked. "I heard you were in town looking for me. I chose not to be found."

"I spoke to his deputy. Asked him to give the envelope and my suspicions to Dawson soon as he returned."

Walker flinched, then regained his arrogant posture. "Good try, Tyler, but I don't believe you." He turned back to Emma. "I have worked too hard to get where I am to lose it now. I want that document. Now." He put the gun to Rafe's head. "Or he dies. You choose."

CHAPTER
Forty-One

T Y WATCHED, POWERLESS TO HELP HIS WIFE WHO SEEMED paralyzed by fear, and unable move.

Walker pushed the gun against Rafe's temple. "You think I won't do it?"

"Don't hurt him! Please! I - I'll do it. Just don't hurt him."

"Just because you get the document back won't end your troubles." Ty stalled for time, feverishly working to loosen the rope around his wrist.

"Ah, but then it will be my word against yours that it ever existed." He actually smiled. "Rafe never saw it. Leo heard him say so. And Emma, well, she didn't want to know what it said." He chuckled at her surprised expression. "You'd be surprised how easy it is find out things around here. Leo, go with her."

The young cowboy looked at Ty and winked. "I'll take real good care of your purty little wife."

Emma nervously licked her lips, then looked at him. The fear he read in her eyes doubled the burning rage he held in check. Seeking to reassure her, he said with deliberate calm. "Don't worry, sweetheart. I'll carve his heart out for you." He nodded toward Walker. "And help you stomp his sorry ass in the dirt."

He saw the steel return and she lifted her chin. "Good." She gave him a tremulous smile and left the room, Leo right behind.

Emma's knees shook as she walked in front of Leo. *I need to get that gun!* She slowed her steps as they entered the office.

"Keep moving!" Leo pushed the barrel into her back.

When she reached the desk, she rested her hip against the edge, laying her hands loosely on either side. "Why, Leo? Why would you do this? I thought you cared for me?"

His face contorted, and he snapped, "I loved you!"

"I didn't know." She brought a hand up, and nervously fingered the top button of her shirt.

He followed each movement with his eyes.

"You never said anything, Leo. I didn't know."

He stiffened as though she struck him. "You knew."

"No, I didn't." She fumbled with the button and it popped open. "If I had known, things could have been so different."

His nostrils flared, and his gaze blazed amber fire. "I would have done anything for you." He took a shuddering breath. "I hated him for putting you out there like some kind of prized heifer. What kind of father does that to his daughter?" He nodded. "I knew you hated it, too, so I had to do something."

"What did you do?" *Do I really want to know?*

"He was supposed to die before we got back."

His casual statement shook her to the core. "What did you do?"

He licked his lips and shuffled his feet, studying the patch of skin visible at the vee of her shirt. "A little arsenic. Just one dose, though. He was so weak that should have done him in quick." He huffed out a breath. "Tough old buzzard."

The lethal calmness in his eyes made her shiver.

"Then you had to go and marry *him*."

He's crazy! I have to keep him talking while I figure out a way out of this! "I had no choice, Leo!" She tried to sound desperate, "If you had just told me how you felt, I could have done things differently."

"I hit him twice, he fell in the water and he *still* didn't die." He adjusted his grip on the gun. "He's got a powerful urge to live." He ogled her chest. "I wonder why?"

Emma's heart pounded and her mouth went dry. She had to get that gun.

There was only one way.

She opened another button. "I can show you why, Leo. But not with a gun in your hand."

He jerked and the weapon pointed down as he sucked in a breath.

"I never knew how much you cared for me, Leo, until now. You're willing to kill for me." She opened her shirt a fraction of an inch. "That's pretty exciting."

"I love you, Emma," he whispered.

"Then show me." She took a step toward him, eyes locked with his. "Put the gun down, and kiss me."

$$\star\ \star\ \star$$

Ty's body throbbed with the sheer force of his anger. He struggled for calm, knowing he needed to keep a clear head.

He focused on Walker. "You don't honestly think this will all just go away."

He relaxed the pressure of the muzzle aimed at Rafe. "Of course it will." He moved away slightly and faced Ty. "Like I said, it will be my word against yours."

The fact that he didn't mention Rafe confirmed what Ty already thought: he planned to kill them all. "I see what your plan was," said Ty.

"Do you, now?" Walker pulled a cigar from his pocket, lowering the gun a little more as he struck a match on the rock mantle. "I'm all ears."

"Your plan to marry Emma yourself fell through since she obviously has good taste."

The other man's tight mouth and narrowed eyes were the only indications Ty's comments hit their mark.

"So you had Leo try to kill me."

"No proof."

"Leo is all the proof I need."

"Providing he's still around, of course." Cold, dead eyes glared back at Ty.

"What would be gained by my death? Rafe would still be here."

"Well, obviously, he wasn't supposed to be."

"You black-hearted son-of-a-bitch!" Rafe bellowed and tried to stand but was overcome by a coughing spell and dropped back into the chair.

Walker watched with dispassionate eyes as the old man

struggled to regain his composure.

The ropes around Ty's hands loosened a little more and the blood slowly began to circulate. "So, with me gone, and Rafe ill, it was only a matter of time before some *accident* took his life, leaving Emma with no one to turn to."

"Such a shame to have that much fire and passion wasted on a man like you." He blew a smoke ring. "But she will come around to my way of thinking. Eventually."

"Will?" His blood ran cold.

"Did I say will?" He chuckled. "Of course, that plan is no longer viable." His brow suddenly furrowed and he looked toward the hall. "What's taking so long? They should have been back by now." He looked at Rafe, then back to Ty as he edged closer to the door, relaxing when he heard footsteps.

The cigar fell from his mouth as Leo walked in, hands clasped over his head, Emma behind him with a .45 in his back.

Too late, Walker brought the barrel of his gun up and swung toward her.

One shot exploded in the tiny room and the lawyer screamed, grabbing his shattered wrist as the gun dropped to the floor.

Leo spun and found the barrel of Emma's gun – his gun – pressed to his heart.

"Go ahead. Move. Please. I want you to."

Ty looked down at his hands, surprised to find the ropes had dropped away. He stood and walked to Emma, nodding toward the gun she held pressed against Leo's chest. "Want me to take that?"

"I'm good. You tie him up. You can get the ropes tighter than me."

He grabbed Leo's arm and shoved him toward the chair he just vacated.

When Wally and José rushed in a few minutes later, they found Ty and Emma in a passionate embrace, Rafe reading by the fireplace, and Leo and Walker trussed up like a Christmas turkey on the floor.

Emma lay pressed against Ty's side, one leg resting on his, fingers smoothing over his chest. "So I just kinda let him think he could kiss me and when he got close enough, I took the gun from him." She lifted a shoulder. "It wasn't too difficult to do." She was silent a moment then continued. "I wasn't sure if you really told that deputy to send the sheriff out or not. I'm glad it wasn't a bluff. I sure wasn't looking forward to having to haul them to town."

"Where'd you learn to shoot like that?"

"Papa taught me." She sighed. "I just wish he'd spent a little time helping me learn woman stuff, too."

His arms tightened and he kissed the top of her head. "You're woman enough for me, Red. Don't ever think otherwise." A soft laugh rumbled through his chest. "Besides, if you were any more of a woman, you'd kill me." His chest rose and fell on a heavy breath. "I'm sorry I wasn't there when you needed me."

She pushed up on one elbow and glared at him. "What the hell does that mean? Of course you were there for me! When you said what you did about cutting out is heart, I knew no matter what, you wouldn't let anything happen to me. That's what gave me the courage to try such a risky stunt."

When he smiled, she felt the full force of the sexual magnetism he exuded, and her breath caught.

He pulled her on top of him, strong hands caressing her back. "Can we make up now?"

His heart pounded slow and steady beneath her hand and she smiled. "I thought you'd never ask."

Epilogue

"Don't make it too high." Emma cautioned, "They're still babies."

Sarah placed a snoozing Abby on the floor beside Little Tyler and took the other rocker. "They've been working on that swing all morning."

"I know," laughed Emma, "Papa and Ty have talked about nothing all week except getting it done." She looked down at her sleeping son. "He's only three months old. It's not like he and Abby will be using it anytime soon."

"I can't believe Rafe is doing so good. Look at him. You'd never know it was less than a year ago, he was at death's door."

"I know. I just thank God he recovered." She shivered as a chill raced over her. "Leo actually tried to poison him with arsenic." She shook her head. "He thought since he was so ill, a little bit would push him over the edge and their plan would work." She wrapped her arms around herself. "It nearly did."

"Prison is too good for both of them." Sarah snapped, "They should've hung for what they did."

"Well, Papa is fine and they won't bother anyone else anytime soon, so let's be happy about that."

"You're right. How's the new house coming? When do you think they will be done with it?"

Emma's smiled returned as she thought of the beautiful home being built on the knoll near the creek. The home her husband was building for them. "Ty said it will be done by the end of summer." Her smile wavered a bit. "I worry about Papa being here all alone but he insisted we needed our own place. And it's not like we won't see him all the time."

"He's right. You need your own place." She looked toward the three grown men taking turns trying out the swing. "You're going to have to have one of those there, too."

"I know."

"What about the cooking lessons?"

"Lupe told me yesterday she'll just do the cooking from now on." Emma snickered. "I'm good at coffee and bacon and eggs, nothing more. She's going to help me find someone for when we move."

Sarah grinned. "But I think you have being a wife and mother down pat."

Emma met Ty's happy gaze. "I thought I didn't know anything about being a woman. Turns out, I know how to love. And that's all there is to it."

THE END

Acknowledgements

While writing itself is pretty much a solitary endeavor, authors require input from a variety of sources to perfect their craft. I owe a huge debt of gratitude to many people as I proudly present my newest work for your reading pleasure.

Authors get inspiration for stories from many sources. For *Groom*, it came from my dear friend and fellow author, Caleb Pirtle, III. Thank you, CP3 for asking me "Why is it always a mail order bride? Why not a mail order groom?" His simple question set off a fire storm of *"what if's"* and Ty and Emma's story was born. I do hope you like the end result.

As always, a huge thank you to my critique partner, who never fails to get me back on track when I get derailed; to my editor for finding the holes I needed to plug; my beta readers for their unfailing loyalty; and to members of my writing groups and a host of friends whose support and encouragement never wavered.

And last, but by no means least, to my family who continually make me believe I can do anything.

About the Author

Awarding winning author Dana Wayne is a sixth generation Texan and resides in the Piney Woods with her husband of 39 years (and counting), a Calico cat named Katie, three children and four grandchildren.

She routinely speaks at book clubs, writers groups and other organizations and successfully coordinated multiple writing events including conferences and workshops as well as appearing on numerous writing blogs.

Her debut contemporary romance, *Secrets of The Heart*, was a 2016 finalist in the ETWG Writing contest, a finalist for the 2017 Scéal Award for Contemporary Romance, Reviewers Top Pick and selected as a Top 10 Books to Read This Winter from Books & Benches online magazine. Her second novel, Mail Order Groom will be available April, 2017.

Affiliations include Romance Writers of America, Texas Association of Authors, Writers League of Texas, East Texas Writers Guild, Northeast Texas Writers Organization, and East Texas Writers Association.

www.danawayne.com

www.Facebook.com/danawayne423

www.Twitter.com/danawayne423

Books by Dana Wayne

Secrets of the Heart
Mail Order Groom

Secrets of the Heart Excerpt
By Dana Wayne

Chapter One

Houston, Texas present day
They died two years ago today.

Tori didn't need the calendar to remember the date. Her heart ticked away the hours one anguished beat at a time then stuttered and skipped each September fourth at 7:01 p.m.; the day her husband and seven year old son were murdered.

She sucked in a lungful of air and forced back the tears threatening to crush her resolve.

No more tears. Time to move forward.

Tori stared at the half-packed suitcase on the bed, each item new and chosen for this journey, symbolic of her mission to start fresh. She was certain her best friend since forever would understand and support her decision. Obviously not the case.

"Oh my God, Tori! Have you lost your mind?" Sasha paced in front of the closet, fingers pressed to her temples. "I am so not believing this!"

Her reaction mirrored the one from Tori's family last night. Going to Montana was one thing, keeping it secret until the night before she left was a lot to accept. Apparently.

Hands on her hips, voice rife with tension, Sassy

- personifying her nickname - raved on. "I mean, really, what do you even know about this guy?" She crossed her arms, right foot tapping out a staccato. "How do you know he's not some wacko serial killer or if he even has a sick mother?"

She didn't give Tori time to take a breath much less respond.

"I can't believe you didn't tell your best friend in the whole world about this hare-brained idea weeks ago instead of the day before you leave."

"You know why." Tori held up her hand. "You're worried, Sassy, I get it. But I have to do this." She placed folded pants in the suitcase and walked back to the closet, staring at the unfamiliar items hanging there. "The past two years have been a never-ending nightmare." She wrapped her arms around herself and struggled to remain calm. "Joey died in my arms." Tori blew out a breath. "I didn't know a human could endure that much pain and live. I never thought their killers would go free, but they did and I survived that, too." Her voice dropped to a soft whisper. "I'm just existing, Sassy. I'm not living anymore."

"Rico is still out there. You know you're a loose end he wants tied up."

"I talked with Captain Lockhart last week and Rico hasn't been seen in months. Word is he took his drug plans elsewhere. Maybe even as far as Canada." She turned back to the closet and pulled a blouse from its hanger, folded it, shook it out then refolded it. "When Joey and Eddie died, a big part of me died, too." She took a breath and tried to speak without crying. "I know I can never get that back. But this job will give me a chance to…re-group, get grounded again."

"But Montana?" Sassy stood in front her. "It's colder 'n

hell there and snows like a gazillion feet a year! What if you need to go to town or get sick or hurt?"

Tori threw the blouse on the bed and faced her friend. "I can't stay here any longer!" She trembled with the effort it took to control the pain that had defined her life the last two years. Eyes blurring with unshed tears, she blinked several times, sucking air through clenched teeth. "Everywhere I go, everyone I see is a constant reminder of all I've lost. And my family, Sassy…they're smothering me."

"They love you. We all do."

She gripped her friends' shoulders. "Then please. For my sake, try to understand. I lost a big piece of myself that day and lose a little more each day I stay here."

Several seconds passed before Sassy placed her hands over Tori's and squeezed. "All right. But promise you'll call if you need anything, anything at all."

"I promise. Now, are you going to help me pack or what?"

"Fine. I'll help, but I want the whole story, start to finish. How the hell did you get hooked up with some cowboy from Montana?"

Tori released a long held breath. "It's not a big deal." She picked up the discarded blouse and refolded it. "Ted Freeman, Chief of Staff at Memorial?"

"Oh yeah, the yummy one that looks like Richard Gere."

She nodded. "He has this friend in Butte who knew about a family, the McBrides' that wanted a live-in nurse for his elderly mother. She has terminal cancer. Pretty advanced."

"They don't have nurses in Montana?"

She ignored the sarcastic comment. "He mentioned it to Ted who mentioned it to me in passing. I asked for more information, made a few calls." Tori shrugged. "And off I go."

Though not that simple, the explanation seemed to satisfy Sasha for now. True, she insisted on a background check and made a few discreet inquiries herself but not until she'd accepted the position. Tori realized significant steps had to take place if she were to have any chance at normal again. This was a significant step. A little rash maybe, but significant, so, no second guessing it now.

It was an ideal solution for her current state of mind. She would live in the McBride home and care for Mr. McBride's sister and mother, receive an acceptable salary, a private room and meals. Most important of all, she'd be free from constant reminders of her loss and well-meaning friends and family – namely her mother - now determined to fix her up with someone.

But she lacked the motivation, and, though loath to admit it, the confidence, to pursue another relationship. Eddie was her first love, and her only lover. Hell, she'd never even kissed another man – not like that - and even the thought of doing so now made her palms sweat and her heart race.

I'm a thirty-three year old coward.

"Hello in there?" Sasha tapped the side of her head. "Anybody home?"

Tori blinked. "Huh?"

"Answer me."

"I'm sorry, my mind was wandering. What did you ask?"

She heaved an exasperated sniff. "I said tell me about this McBride fella. What does he look like, is he married? And I want the good stuff, too, not whatever sugar-coated version you gave your parents."

Tori hesitated.

Sasha poked her shoulder with her index finger. "Out

with it. What are you hiding?"

"Nothing." She studied the closet's contents without seeing them. "There isn't much to tell. He runs the family ranch. His brother was the sheriff before he and his wife were killed three months ago." She took a sweater and studied it. "That's about it."

"And you never met 'im?"

"Uh-uh, just spoke with him on the phone. Got the majority of my information from his sister, Sheila. She had some sort of accident, too and needs PT."

"Okay then, what does he sound like? Old? Sexy? Gay?"

"You're incorrigible."

"Well?"

"I guess…hell, I don't know." She swapped the sweater for blouse. "It's hard to describe." *Liar. You know exactly how it sounds; a deep baritone with a huskiness to it that flows through you like fine wine, raises gooseflesh on your arms, leaving you off-balance, a strange tingling sensation racing through you.* She placed a hand at her throat and tried to breathe normally as guilt over such forbidden feelings overwhelmed her. *If just the sound of his voice on the phone has such an effect on me, what on earth will happen when I meet him?*

"Dammit! You're not listening again."

The declaration, complete with a heavy sigh, pulled Tori from those disturbing thoughts. "I'm sorry. What did you say?"

Sasha rolled her eyes and made no attempt to hide her frustration. "I said, give it to me."

"Give what?"

"I know good and well you at least got a picture of him before sashaying across the country to meet him, so gimmee."

She looked away, said nothing.

Her best friend held out her hand and snapped her fingers. "Hand it over, girl. I wanna see the man who could persuade my reasonably intelligent – "

"Reasonably intelligent?"

Sasha cocked her head to the side, one delicately arched brow raised.

"Point made."

"As I was saying, persuade my reasonably intelligent best friend to hightail it to Montana in the dead of winter." She wiggled her fingers and grinned. "I can't wait to see him."

Tori glanced at the outstretched hand and reached for her purse. She didn't bother to glance at the photo as she passed it over; didn't need to. Her mind's eye provided a vivid picture. Wind-blown ebony hair, streaks of grey at the temples. Strong, defined cheekbones anchored by heavy brows. Sky blue eyes framed by killer lashes. And his mouth. Oh God. What was it about his mouth that intrigued her so?

Full lips parted in a sexy smile that lit up his face and made her breath catch. She gave herself a mental shake and tried to focus on the task at hand. "His sister sent it. He's the one on the left. The other one is his late brother, Isaac."

"Holy-moly girlfriend! No wonder you can't wait to go. Talk about your tall, dark and handsome. He's what…six feet at least; bedroom eyes if ever I saw 'em, come hither smile… daaa-yum! I bet he's got a killer ass, too."

"Sassy!" Tori reached for the picture but her friend moved away, still studying it.

"What did you say his name is?"

"Wade McBride."

"Well, Mr. Wade McBride, you are one delicious lookin'

cowboy." She made a show of fanning herself with the picture. "And I'd be on 'at puppy like mornin' glory on a fencepost."

Her face grew warm and she shook her head. Sasha had a one track mind of late and did her best to get Tori on the same track.

"Damn. Damn. Damn!" She handed the picture back. "Sure you don't want me to come along? You're a bit out of practice you know, and he may be more than you can handle alone."

"It's nothing like that and you know it. It's a job."

"Yeah, well, it should be." She rummaged through the contents of a dresser drawer and tossed a filmy nightgown at Tori. "Better take this along. Winter or not you'll want it 'fore this is over."

"Good grief! Is sex all you think about?" She tossed the garment back to her and pulled out a pair of sweat pants.

"Hell yeah when I see a Timex man."

Tori ducked her head and sighed. "I know I will regret this, but…a Timex man?"

Sasha giggled. "Think a can of RediWhip topping, some chocolate syrup…a strategically placed cherry." She paused for effect. "And see if 'at cowboy can take a lickin' and keep on tickin.'"

Her face flamed as an image of McBride lathered in whipped topping and chocolate syrup formed. "Oh my God, Sasha! Where on earth do you come up with this stuff?" She extended her arm, palm up. "Never mind. I don't want to know."

"Trust me…one day you'll thank me."

"No. I won't. Besides, he has a lot on his plate with his sister and mother both ill and the ranch. He needs a nurse, not a lover."

"Says who?"

"Sassy, please."

"I've said it before and I'll say it again; you were too good for Eddie." She waved her hand back and forth to silence Tori's rebuke. "I know, I know, it's wrong to speak ill of the dead. He was a good cop, a decent father, but a crummy, cheating husband."

Tori sat on the edge of the bed and said nothing as her friend continued. "You've got the kindest heart of anyone I've ever known." Sassy joined her on the bed, her smile reflective. "I guess that explains why you put up with me all these years. And you have a capacity for caring I truly envy. It's why you are such an awesome nurse. Well, that and the reasonably intelligent thing."

Tori snorted. Sassy would never change. Thank God.

"I know you loved Eddie. I never understood why, but I know you did. But he's gone, Tori. You need to let him go and love again."

"I...I don't know if I can. Every time I think about moving on, of getting involved with someone, I feel guilty. Like I'm...betraying him. I know it sounds silly to you but it's how I feel."

Sasha slid an arm around her shoulders and squeezed. "I don't think it sounds silly at all. He was your husband and you loved him. But he's gone." She blew out a breath. "You're my best friend in the whole world. I want you to be happy. I want to see your eyes smile again."

"I know you do. And I appreciate that." She leaned her head on her friend's shoulder. "I'm not interested in a relationship right now." She sighed. "I don't think I even remember how to kiss anymore so a relationship is out of the question."

Sasha looked at the picture and grinned. "Wanna bet? Besides, kissing is like riding a bike, once you do it, you don't forget how." She giggled. "And if you did, I'm bettin' this cowboy is one hell of a teacher."

Tori placed the last bag on the cart by the door and called for a taxi. She stood in the middle of her living room, staring at the expensive set of matching luggage she'd splurged on, mentally checking off her preparations. Her rent was paid up for six months and the mail forwarded to her parents who would take care of any bills. Her friend had a key to the apartment and would keep an eye on things while she was gone.

She suffered no misgivings about leaving. In fact, her excitement grew as departure time approached. The need to take control of her life was of major importance right now. When she heard about the McBride's needing a nurse, it was like a rainbow following a thunderstorm proclaiming the worst was over.

Maybe it was the prospect of change itself making her tingle with anticipation or something else altogether. Wade's enticing voice notwithstanding, exactly what pulled her to Montana remained a mystery. She only knew she had to go.

The doorman rang to say the taxi arrived. Tori grabbed her purse, the cumbersome luggage cart and headed out the door. As it shut, she heard the phone ring.

She let it go to voicemail.

www.ingramcontent.com/pod-product-compliance
Lightning Source LLC
Chambersburg PA
CBHW032116180726
48284CB00002B/585